37 DAYS TO DESTINY

J A SMITH
WITH
CURTIS SMITH

Dear Gina & Trisha,
Enjoy!
Judy

Jim + Trisha,
I hope you like it.
Curtis

37 DAYS TO DESTINY

Copyright © 2014 by Jodi Watters

37 DAYS TO DESTINY – Copyright © 2015 by J. A. Smith

All rights reserved. Without limiting the rights under copyright reserved above, no part of this publication may be reproduced, stored in or introduced into a retrieval system, or transmitted, in any form, or by any means (electronic, mechanical, photocopying, recording, or otherwise) without the prior written permission of both the copyright owner and the above publisher of this book.

This is a work of fiction. Names characters, places, and incidents are the product of the author's imagination. Any other likeness to actual events is coincidental other than brief quotations from the King James Version of the Bible.

Formatting by (http://wildseasformatting.com/)

Acknowledgements

Thanks to a very encouraging family who were there for us from the very beginning of *37 Days To Destiny*. It would have been much harder if we had to do it without you.

A special thanks goes to Heather A. Ewalt, who did a thorough edit, and to Krystal G. Scarbrough for her wise input regarding content changes.

To Stephen T. Scarbrough, a sincere thank you for the wonderful cover art you created while on your mission furlough from Thailand.

To our many friends, your special input has been appreciated. You've always been positive, encouraging, supportive and we send our undying thanks.

37 DAYS TO DESTINY

CHARACTERS

Andy Warren - Hit & Run victim; Importer of fine antiques
Jim Redmon; wife Beth - P.I. from Chattanooga
Philip Warren - Andy's uncle
Andy's Pall Bearers -Buddies from Army
    Jerry Smith
    Paul Masters
    Carlos Santiago
    Butch Lawson - Computer guru
    David Weintroub - DEA agent
Rebecca Langley - Andy's girlfriend
Detective Bob Stevens - N.Y. Homicide detective
Fred Houseman - Owner of Houseman Galleries
Bruce Foster - FBI agent
Manny Randolf - Hired driver for Jim
Ralph Mercer - Property desk officer
Mandy - Nurse at safe house
Lockman - Houseman's Warehouse Supervisor
Ali Madur - Member of radical Muslim group
Sven Abadi - Member of radical Muslim group
Ahmed Abadi - Sven's father
Jamaal - Cabbie & Ahmed's best friend
Katarina Knutzen Abadi - Ex-wife of Abadi; Sven's mother
Gofar Hakimi - Sven's best friend

1.
The Funeral

The February day was overcast with a light rain promising to turn to snow and the cold seemed to penetrate and send a chill to the bones. It was dismal for eleven in the morning, which made it seem like seven at night; a perfect day for a sad funeral.

Inside the small Catholic Church, amongst the mourners, were a number of single ladies sniffling into their hankies. Not one could believe that their beloved Andy Warren was really gone. The truth of it would have been more believable if there had been an open casket, but the authorities said the body was unfit for viewing because of the head injuries.

After the Mass, close friends and relatives were invited to offer a short tribute about the man lying in the closed coffin at the foot of the steps. The first to speak was the childless loving uncle who was like a second father to the deceased. He brought Andrew into his import business as a kind gesture to his dead brother, and he spoke with admiration about how talented and successful his nephew had become. After the emotional elderly man concluded his remarks, he made his way back to the pew.

The next person to speak was Jim Redmon, the deceased's friend and ex-captain in the army. Jim explained how close their squad had become and shared some of the funny things Andy had said and done over the years. He explained to everyone how their group continued to get together regularly and how it had cemented their friendships. Jim had the crowd laughing one minute and the next they were in tears. He concluded his eulogy by saying how much Andy would be missed.

The last person to share was a strikingly beautiful lady who was dressed in the latest fashion and carried herself like a model. You could tell she had *class* from the moment she rose out of her seat to walk forward

The woman spoke quietly and was eloquent. "Andy Warren was the one everyone wanted to be with." Her voice slipped into a tone of confidentiality as she continued, "It didn't matter that you weren't the only woman in his life, but what really mattered was he had chosen *you* to be on his arm for the evening. You wouldn't even consider declining his invitation, for an evening with Andy always promised to be interesting and fun." Many of the women nodded their heads, wiping an occasional tear. "You see, Andy had the gift of being able to make the person he was with to feel as if they were the most important person in the world!" The remark brought several knowing nods.

She went on, staring out over the crowd recalling an incident. "Several years ago, I recall going to dinner with Andy and a group of his friends. He whispered into my ear that he was going to ask the piano player to play my favorite song and slipped away from the table. As he waited for the pianist to finish his set, a woman approached and casually spoke to him. Always a gentleman, he nodded and returned his attention to the musician waiting for a break in the music; at which time he made his request and returned to our table.

"It was with surprise that a rather drunk man approached our table and grabbed Andy by the shoulder. He blustered he wouldn't stand for him making a play for his girl right in front of everyone...and if Andy didn't think he meant business, he would see him outside! To make his point, with a flourish, the man opened his jacket to reveal a revolver." She paused to let the reality sink in and could see she had everyone's rapt attention. "Andy slowly rose to his feet, and with a smile, explained that he had never seen the man's lady friend in his life and had simply agreed with her when she complimented the pianist. Furthermore he had more than enough to handle with the beautiful lady with him...at which point he kindly gestured toward me. The man wouldn't let it lie and his threats became louder. Andy politely opened the left side of *his* jacket and revealed that he, too, had a gun. He spoke into the man's ear and the man turned on his heel and we never saw or heard from him again. When questioned, Andy wouldn't tell us what he said to the man. 'It's not important,' he said, 'Let's have a good time and forget it.'

She became silent for a moment. "As most of you know, Andy had the 'gift' to diffuse volatile situations with a smile, but he wasn't afraid of a fight either." She looked out over the mourners motioning to the casket. "I'm sure everyone in this church could share an interesting story about Andy, but I learned something new about him that particular evening: he treasured life but never backed down if he knew he was on the side of right." She paused. "He was a very special man and I loved him dearly." Her eyes blurred as she regally made her way to her pew followed by complete silence in the church.

The service continued and soon Andy's six army friends solemnly made their way to the front. They each took their place beside the casket preparing to carry their dear friend to the hearse waiting outside. The family followed after them, some stopping briefly to speak to the priest.

After the congregation left, the wives of Jim Redmon, Paul Masters, Jerry Smith, and Carlos Santiago, headed for a car waiting for them. Before Beth Redmon got in their car, she approached the beautiful lady who had offered the eulogy at the service.

"I'm so glad you shared such a meaningful story about Andy." Beth offered her hand and the woman clasped it. "I'm Beth Redmon, the wife of one of Andy's army buddies that served as a pall bearer today." She paused as she looked into the woman's eyes. "If you're going to the cemetery, you're welcome to ride with us." The woman was pleased and the two approached the car.

After settling into the limo, the woman said, "I appreciate being asked to ride with you. Andy spoke of his army friends frequently; he considered each and every one of them like a brother." As she glanced around the car, she introduced herself, "My name is Rebecca Langley."

All the passengers introduced themselves and Beth reached over and patted Rebecca's hand, "Andy obviously meant a lot to you, and I'm sure the feeling was mutual." Rebecca reached for her hankie and dabbed at her beautiful green eyes, which reminded Beth of two large emeralds. Andy's lady friend quickly stared out the window as the limo merged into traffic.

2.
The Wake

After the graveside service, Mr. Warren invited some business friends and the pall bearers and spouses to Andy's apartment. His apartment was spectacular with many valuable paintings displayed, as well as collectibles and statuary sprinkled throughout. His uncle was based in California and was staying there since Andy's death. His wife had died years before and now Andy was gone. The only close relative he had was a wayward niece somewhere in the mid-west and he hadn't had contact with her for over ten years.

Rebecca Langley was also at the Wake, and she seemed right at home. Beth sensed a friendly connection between her and Andy's uncle; she was relaxed and seemed in a familiar element. Both women seemed to gravitate toward one another and Beth started the conversation by asking her how she met Andy.

"Six months after I was divorced, I bought an apartment in Manhattan. I decided to decorate it to suit *me*, and I started looking at things in upscale antique shops. (My ex-husband had always insisted on modern furniture with monochromatic whites and beiges until I thought I'd go nuts.) So I was looking for a few interesting pieces to sprinkle throughout my *colorful* apartment. You can believe I didn't paint anything white but the wood trim!" she said with a smile.

Rebecca continued, "Andy was in one of the shops I was visiting. He was there on business and was waiting for the owner to finish with a customer. He started browsing and noticed my interest in a small sculpture. He wandered over and asked me if I liked the piece. I told him very much, but actually I was far more interested in him. He was handsome and pleasant and was the first man I had seen since my divorce that I thought I'd like to meet."

Beth's curiosity soared but she held her tongue.

"He enlightened me about the piece I was looking at and gave me some tips about what to look for when shopping for antiques. He looked at his watch and asked me if I'd like to join him for a cup of coffee at the café across the street.

"At that point, I'd have gone to Yankee Stadium with him, and I don't even like baseball! So he interrupted the manager explaining he'd be back and we left. It was the beginning of the most exciting romance you can imagine. It didn't take me long to realize that Andy wasn't settling down with anyone, and if I wanted to enjoy the ride, I'd have to accept it. It was good timing for me because I was still smarting from the heartbreak after my husband of ten years decided he didn't love me anymore. She shook her head, looking shyly at Beth. "I can't believe I'm telling you all this, and I hardly know you!"

Beth smiled, "I think it's easier to open up to a total stranger than an old friend who's been through the 'muck' with you. I have a strong marriage and Jim and I are still in love. It's a different kind of love than when we were first married; now it's a deeper trusting love."

"Do you realize how unusual that is? After seven years, my husband still wanted the party life, fast cars, trips, and no kids to complicate things. Don't get me wrong, I enjoyed the partying and all to a certain extent, I was just ready to settle down and have a family; my biological clock was ticking." She looked past Beth, remembering. "It was right after I begged him to consider starting a family when he told me it was over." She paused. "I never want to live through a time like that again."

Beth knew she had to change the subject fast. This woman had suffered two hard losses in a very short time. "Rebecca, would you find it too hard to tell me what actually happened to Andy? We've only gotten bits and pieces from his uncle but hesitate to bring it up again tonight."

Rebecca nodded, agreeing. "I know recently Andy was going back and forth to London and Paris more than usual. I asked him about it, and he just brushed it off as nothing unusual. He said the import business sometimes went in spurts so I dropped the questions. Recently, I knew Andy was ready to open his own antique shop and even invited me to look at some places with him. He finally settled on one. He seemed glad that he wouldn't have to go on buying trips as often except when he wanted something special.

"I noticed Andy wasn't sleeping well and just assumed it was because he had a lot on his mind with the new shop. I tried to get him to talk to me about it but he let me know it wasn't anything serious. Anyway, I knew something wasn't right but felt like if he wanted to talk, he knew where to find me."

The young woman's eyes blurred with tears. "I think I could have helped him, if only to be a good and trusted listener." She made a determined effort to gain control. "You know, Beth, I loved him so much and I think he loved me, but for some reason he couldn't commit. It was beginning to become harder and harder for me to be with him and still be on the outside."

"It would be extremely hard; I'm sure you cried yourself to sleep many a night."

Rebecca was surprised that Beth had understood so completely. She started to share something else, but Jim came over to capture his wife and led her over to speak with Mr. Warren. *None too soon,* thought Rebecca, *it's insane how much I told her!"*

Their whole squad was able to attend Andy's funeral and Jim reserved a block of rooms at a nice, respectable hotel that Dave used when he was in New York. Luckily, it was within walking distance of the church.

Jim wanted all of the pall bearers to be in the same hotel so they could get together Saturday evening. All the couples had a room of their own. The single guys, Dave Weintroub and Butch Lawson, shared a room. Sadly, Butch and his wife had recently divorced and Dave had remained single. All were pleasantly surprised when the Redmons picked up the tab for the rooms. It never failed to amaze them their ex-captain was a multi-millionaire and was always generous.

Jim had a suite for Beth and himself, which included a spacious sitting room. The Redmons invited all their friends to join them Saturday evening for a time of sharing memories. After they met, they talked about the day's activities and Beth told them about her chat with Rebecca. "I believe she knows more than she realizes. I think she was about to say more when Jim interrupted us and led me away." Jim looked at her sheepishly.

Butch piped up, "I never believed for a minute Andy's death was an accident! He was way too sharp to drink that much and go out on the street. He talked to me plenty about getting my act together when I was in the sauce, so I think it's a stretch to think he was in a drunken state when the car hit him."

Paul and Janie Masters sat close by listening intently. He was settled quite well in a job as an Inspector with the Detroit Police Department and offered to see if he could find out anything for Jim.

Sunday morning dawned and soon everyone was drifting down

to breakfast. They revisited the ideas they'd had the night before. Jim planned to call Mr. Warren and invite him to lunch. He thought it would be interesting to get his take on things.

As offered, Paul said he'd call the police department when he got home. He had a friend on the force who had moved to New York years before and may still be with the NYPD. He'd like to locate him and see if he'd be willing to do some digging for the cause.

The group agreed to pack and meet for coffee early the next morning. Some of them had to leave. Jim was thinking what most of them were thinking: *At the last reunion, we never realized it would be the last time we would see Andy.*

3.
Plans

The Redmons entered the cozy restaurant looking around to see if Andy's uncle had arrived yet. The elderly man stood and waved them over to a booth. He and Jim shook hands, and Beth gave him a hug.

"We're so glad you could join us, Mr. Warren. We just have so many questions and didn't want to leave New York without some answers." Jim unfolded his napkin, and looked at him. "This may seem insensitive, but are you satisfied with what the police have told you?"

"No, not at all," he said. "Andrew wasn't one to be out walking around at ten at night; especially inebriated! From what I know, there were no restaurants or bars in that vicinity and it wasn't near his apartment. For the life of me, I can't figure out why he was in that area!"

The waitress approached and the threesome gave her their drink orders. She moved on and they looked at their menus. After a short time, Jim put his down and started his probing.

"How did you find out Andy was dead?" he questioned.

"Well, I was just finishing some paperwork and intended to call a friend for dinner when the phone rang. It was the NYPD inquiring if I was Andrew's uncle. He said he had bad news; Andrew had been involved in a hit-and-run accident and had just died in the ambulance on the way to the hospital! Needless to say, it was shocking and I had to sit down to take it all in. He was the son I never had; the grief that assailed me could not have been worse if he *were* my son!" Mr. Warren looked beyond them, remembering his nephew.

Drawing the man back to the present, Jim gently asked, "At that time, did they say anything more about the accident?"

"No, but I asked if they had apprehended the driver of the car. They said no, that no one had come forward, and there were no witnesses to date. They said the story had appeared on TV, on the eleven o'clock news, and in the newspaper, but no calls had come in as of yet. I told them I'd be in New York as soon as I could book a flight, and they gave me a number to call when I arrived. The minute I walked into Andrew's apartment, I called them."

The waitress delivered their drinks and took their orders. After she left, Jim asked, "Was his shop anywhere near there?"

"No, it wasn't close in proximity to the accident." Mr. Warren was surprised Jim knew about it. "Andrew asked I not mention he had leased a place with an option to purchase, which I didn't, not even to the police. I knew there was something amiss if he was privately contemplating such an important move, but he didn't share it with me. And to answer your question, I believe the awful thing that happened to Andrew had something to do with his business. By filling in the blanks from some of our conversations, I think he ran up against something or someone unpleasant. For some reason, he didn't want to share, and believe me I gave him ample opportunity. I wish I had pushed the subject and got him to confide in me." The man shook his head, "Too late now."

"Mr. Warren, Andy and I didn't stay in touch very often but I did get a surprise call from him about a month ago. After telling me about his renting his own shop, I felt he was skirting an issue and it was like he was trying to decide if he should say more. In the end, we just made small talk and he never opened up; so he never confided in me either."

"I know Andrew thought highly of you, Jim. He told me many stories about you and the squad and how much he regarded all of you. There is one thing I feel I should tell you, I do know that he became interested in Rebecca Langley more than any other lady he had ever dated. She was the one who spoke at the funeral; a very lovely woman."

Beth said, "I talked with her briefly at the Wake and I agree. She was about to tell me something when we were interrupted and I got the distinct impression she was glad we were."

Mr. Warren spoke thoughtfully. "I think Andrew was seriously considering something more permanent with Rebecca. He never said so, but I could read him pretty well. I think it would be beneficial for you to talk with her at length. Perhaps she would feel comfortable opening up to you."

Jim nodded, thinking, *I'm way ahead of you, Mr. Warren.*

The meal arrived and the threesome enjoyed their tasty lunch. When it came time to leave, Mr. Warren asked, "Jim, would you consider staying on in New York awhile and look into this for me?

You're welcome to stay at Andrew's apartment." He looked Beth's way and added, "As you well know, they have some outstanding museums, theaters and shopping here. If Jim accepts my offer, I'm sure you could keep busy if you'd consider staying."

Once again, Mr. Warren directed his attention to Jim. "I have to go back to California in the morning. I have some important meetings scheduled that I postponed because of Andrew's death. I know this may be way too presumptuous of me to ask, but I'm not a bit satisfied with what the police seem to believe."

Jim thanked him for his offer and agreed they'd consider it. "Right now, would it be okay to go back to Andy's and look through his apartment? No telling what I might find. By the way, did Andy ever tell you what I do for a living?"

"Yes sir, he did, and that is exactly why I thought it would be a good idea to have you look into this for me. I need a good detective who can investigate this case and not have their time split with other cases. I know the police have good intentions but they just don't have the time to give it as much attention as I'd like. Of course, I'll pay you whatever you charge. I'd like to think I had someone working on Andrew's case who really cared about him." The elderly man sighed. "Will you let me know as soon as you make a decision?"

Mr. Warren hailed a cab and took Jim and Beth back to Andy's apartment. When they entered, the place had been tossed! Jim went into *work mode* immediately. He checked to see if the door had been forced and found that whoever entered, had a key or were very slick thieves.

Jim quietly told Mr. Warren and Beth not to go any further. "I'd better call the police!" he declared. As they returned to the entry hall, Jim inquired, "Mr. Warren, do you have the number of the cop who called you in California?"

The man checked his wallet and produced a piece of paper with the number on it. "Here it is," he said, as he handed it over. Jim placed the call to Officer James Hunter and waited for the man to answer. He explained he was one of Andrew Warren's pall bearers and he and his wife had come back to the apartment with Andrew's uncle after lunch. Jim told him what they had discovered.

Officer Hunter asked, "How long will you be there, Mr. Redmon?"

"I'd be happy to wait if you're coming right over."

"Me and my partner are on our way."

"We'll go down and wait for you in the lobby," offered Jim.
"Good idea," said Hunter.

4.
Investigation

As they waited, Jim asked Mr. Warren more questions. "Did you get an opportunity to go through any of Andy's things before the funeral?"

"I only glanced at surface papers lying on top of his desk. There was nothing of interest; just bills, a lease, and some sales receipts." The old gentleman paused. "I didn't look through any of his personal items in the bedroom; it was too painful."

"Did you answer his phone at all?"

"He didn't have a land-line; just a cell and I'm sure the police have it. They said they'd return everything after their investigation was over."

"Was Andy robbed?" asked Jim.

"No. His wallet and valuables were still on him. Those items were how they identified Andrew. They told me it would be better if I didn't see him like that."

Just then, a young man entered the front door and made his way around the back of the reception desk in the lobby. Jim approached him, offering his hand, "I'm Jim Redmon, and I was one of Andrew Warren's friends."

The man shook hands saying, "I was sorry to hear about his death; he was a stand-up guy." He then held up a lunch bag. "I don't get a lunch hour; so I usually have something delivered or go out." He was on the defensive. "I've only been gone about 20 or 30 minutes."

Jim doubted the guy was *ever* permitted to leave the building for lunch. At this point, he could care less. His boss he was not! He asked, "Did anyone use the elevators before you left?"

He squinted his eyes, thinking. "Come to think of it, right after the gentleman left, two guys entered I'd never seen before. They obviously had a key fob for the front door so I didn't think anything about it. After they came in, they went straight to the elevators."

"Did you happen to notice what floor they went to?"

"No, sorry, I didn't. I was thinking about other things." He had a thoughtful expression cross his face, "But I do remember they were only in the building for about an hour. Strange looking birds," he added.

"How so?"

"One of them had a suit and tie on and the other was in jeans and leather jacket. Why are you asking me all these questions?" he asked.

"We just came from lunch with Mr. Warren, Andrew's uncle, and found the apartment had been ransacked. It's a mess. If the two strangers you described had anything to do with it, you've given us a good lead!"

The guy beamed, seeming to understand the importance of what he'd witnessed. "I'll help you guys any way I can. Do you want me to call the police?"

"I called them from the apartment. They're on their way and we expect them any minute. Before I let you get back to your lunch, do you recall if they got in a car, and if so can you give me a description?"

Once again, a look of concentration crossed the man's face before he spoke. "Yeah, they got into a Mercedes, and I remember it because it was too cool; brand new! It was dark blue with a light interior. A guy with a beard was seated at the wheel and it was parked at the curb. I remember thinking, 'How stupid is that?' with cops patrolling our building all the time."

Jim filed the information away in his mind. "You've been an amazing witness and I sure appreciate your help. If you think of anything else, give me a call." He handed the man one of his cards.

"So you're a detective as well as his friend?"

"Absolutely, and I want you to know I believe I'll be hanging around for awhile." With that said, he glanced at Beth to get her take on it.

She smiled slyly at him and whispered, "The minute we saw Andy's apartment, I knew you'd take the case!" He grinned back at her.

While the threesome waited on the police, Jim asked Mr. Warren if he'd mind giving him legal authorization to pick up Andy's belongings since he wouldn't be there. He said his permission would have to be notarized and he was sure they could get it done at their hotel in the morning. Mr. Warren assured him he'd take care of it.

Within moments, the police arrived. After shaking hands and introductions, they all entered an elevator and glided up to the tenth floor.

Mr. Warren produced the apartment key and allowed the police to enter. After they glanced into the living room and saw the chaos, they drew Jim and Mr. Warren aside and asked them to remain in the entryway. Jim asked if they could grab a couple of bar stools for Beth and Mr. Warren and they were only too glad to oblige.

"What about you? You want a stool, too?" the officer asked.

Jim shook his head and drew Hunter aside and explained to him that he was a PI and had just been retained by Mr. Warren because he wasn't satisfied with the accident theory. "Would it be too much if I asked to look over your shoulder while you check the crime scene? I promise I won't touch anything or get in your way."

Hunter thought it over, mentioned the request to his partner, and they agreed to allow Jim to watch the proceedings.

As the men started their investigation, Jim was pleased to witness their thoroughness. When they looked at Andy's desk, he practically salivated when he saw the lease. He hoped they wouldn't bag it because he wanted to check the document and the location of the proposed property. As the officers left the room, Jim slyly slipped his cell phone out and took a picture of the top page.

The police went into Andy's bedroom and saw the mattress was askew, the pillows were slit, the pictures were crooked, and drawers were dumped upside down on the bed. Everything within sight had been thoroughly searched.

Jim stuck his head into the bathroom and saw that the vanity had been emptied as well as the linen closet.

That left the kitchen; it was a disaster! Jim couldn't believe the mess. Every box of crackers, cereal, and coffee were upended. The freezer had been emptied, including the ice container. There was food and dishes strewn all over the place. *I don't believe they missed anything,* was Jim's first thought, *but I don't think they found what they were looking for.*

Hunter remarked, "Whatever these guys wanted, I don't think they found it. We didn't find a safe or anything looking like a key to a safe. Which reminds me, I don't think there was a set of keys on the body. If this isn't a hit-and-run crime, that explains how the apartment door wasn't forced; they probably used a key. This is looking more and more like a well-planned homicide rather than a robbery!"

Hunter pulled out his cell and called headquarters. "I'm at the Warren apartment and this may be a murder we're investigating. Better call in Homicide." He gave them the address and asked Jim and company to go back to the lobby once again; he was sure a detective would want to ask them some questions.

The police asked Mr. Warren to stay out of the apartment until their investigation was over; all he could take were his personal things. With the cop looking over his shoulder, he managed to identify his shaving equipment and clothing, then left. Jim and Beth were still waiting in the lobby.

"I called our hotel to make sure we could extend our reservation if needed and made a reservation for you tonight." Jim advised.

"I thank you. And don't you think it's time you called me by my given name? I'm Philip and would be pleased for both of you to call me that." The older man smiled.

Jim nodded, and added, "If you'll give me a minute, I want to ask the doorman a few more questions." As Beth and Mr. Warren waited out front, he approached the young man and asked, "Could you describe the men you saw enter the building after Mr. Warren left"?

"The guy in jeans was a bald guy, about 5' 10" and was built like a wrestler; also his neck was covered with tats. The guy in the suit was a little shorter and partially bald. He was well-built too, with an olive complexion but that's about all I can tell you. I never really looked them in the face."

"Thanks, buddy. You're very observant and I'd appreciate it if you'd keep an eye out. . .especially if that twosome returns." Jim paused, "The police upstairs asked us to wait in the lobby for a detective, but we need to leave. Could you have him call us if he has questions for us?"

"You got it. I have your card right here," he said as he held it up.

Jim stepped outside and hailed a taxi.

"Now what?" asked Beth. "Being a woman, and since I'm eventually going to be staying there, I wonder who is going to take care of the mess?"

"Oh they'll sift every bit of evidence they can find; take pictures, have multiple conferences and then let Mr. Warr...*Philip* know when they're finished. Then I get to go through everything for my own investigation. After that, we hire a service to come in and clean it. It could take awhile so I'm glad we've hung on to our hotel accommodations."

Pleasure crossed Philip's face. "It sounds like you have a plan already. You know I'd like to stay, but my flight leaves tomorrow morning. When I get back to California, I need to prepare for my meetings." The gentleman paused, "Before I forget, please add the up-coming hotel expenses to my bill! No telling how long it'll be before you and Beth can move in there." The man pulled out his check book and said, "I'm writing you a check as a retainer to cover anything additional you might need."

Jim held up a restraining hand, "No need. I'll bill you when I'm finished."

Later, Beth suggested she keep her flight reservation. "I think I should go home and get some things if we're going to be here for an extended time. I'll be back as soon as I can."

5.
Departures and Lists

At 7 a.m. Monday morning, Philip Warren joined Beth and Jim for breakfast.

His whole demeanor seemed to speak of how pleased he was with Jim's decision to take Andrew's case. Jim shared some of his plans, and soon they parted with Philip going back to his room to get his luggage and the notarized letter.

Beth and the Santiago's shared a cab to the airport. After they left, Jim went back to the room. He had a million thoughts going through his mind and, as usual, decided to make a list of his priorities. He sat at the desk in his suite and pulled out the hotel's stationery.
   1. Call Raiders and Rebecca Langley
   2. Call Hunter for permission to go to Warren apartment
   . Who is head detective on case?
   . When can I get Andy's cell and personal effects back?
   3. Check picture of Lease for address
   . Make appointment to see Andy's shop
   4. Go to site of hit-and-run

His first call was to Paul and he reported that he hadn't received a call-back from his friend from the NYPD. If he didn't hear by the end of the day, he promised to call again the following morning; his plane was boarding in minutes.

When he spoke with Butch, he reminded Jim how odd it was when Rebecca said Andy was carrying a gun. "Do you ever remember Andy packing?" he asked.

"Never."

"Looks like you have a real live mystery on your hands, Captain. Wish I could be there to help. If you need anything, call me."

Beth, Carlos and his wife had just arrived at JFK Airport. After Carlos heard what was going on, he offered to help Beth in any way he could when they got back to Chattanooga, including driving her back to the airport for her return to New York.

Dave had business in New York and was still in town. Jim was only mildly surprised because he knew Dave's job with the DEA didn't allow him to discuss his cases. The two made plans to have dinner that evening.

Jerry and spouse were driving back as they planned to make several stops. Jerry was good about keeping up with the men who were trying to get their lives back on track after graduating from his second-chance wilderness camp.

Jim crossed "call raiders" off his list. Next he decided to call Rebecca. *That should get me started,* thought Jim. *There is so much no one knows: I never realized how private Andy was. Who were his friends? Did he confide in anyone? What restaurants did he frequent? I'm sure Rebecca can answer some of those questions and I'll try to get with her tomorrow.*

"Hi Rebecca, this is Jim Redmon."

"Well hello! Are you still in town?"

"Yes I am. Beth is flying back home this morning and will be returning later this week. I've been hired by Philip Warren to look into Andy's case."

"That gives me a great deal of peace," she said.

"Beth and I accompanied Philip back to Andy's apartment yesterday afternoon, and we discovered someone had broken into his apartment. Everything was torn up! When the police give me permission, I'd like you to go over there with me; I'd never know if something was missing."

The woman was surprised. "It's inconceivable that someone broke into his apartment; they have pretty tight security there! I'll be happy to go with you, Jim. I have some tentative plans this week, so if you'd give me a heads up I'll try to rearrange my schedule."

"Of course," he paused, "Would you be available to have lunch with me on Thursday to just answer some questions?"

"Glad to. Since you're a stranger here, do you want me to suggest a place?"

"That'd be great. I'd prefer to go to a place that you and Andy frequented, if that wouldn't be too painful for you."

"No. I'm alright. The sorrow assails me when I least expect it; so it doesn't matter where I am." She then described a restaurant not too far from Andy's apartment and set a time to meet Jim there.

Now for number two on my list, determined Jim.

Officer Hunter answered his phone after three rings. "Hunter here."

Jim explained why he was calling and the cop explained it was too early to give permission to enter the apartment. Jim again explained that Philip Warren had retained him as a Private Investigator for the case and he'd like to get started as soon as possible.

"I understand your hurry, but that's all I can tell you. A detective has been assigned the case and I'm out of the loop."

"Would you give me his name and number?" asked Jim.

"Sure. Just a minute."

After he got the number, Jim asked Hunter if he knew how he could quickly get a permit to carry a concealed weapon. Hunter told him he didn't know off the top of his head but suggested Jim call the front desk of any police station for that information.

As soon as the two ended their call, Jim called the homicide detective immediately.

"Detective Stevens," the man barked into the phone.

Whoops, thought Jim, *not a good day; better tread lightly.*

"Detective Stevens, this is Jim Redmon. I'm calling about the Warren case. Philip Warren has hired me as his liaison with the police department to get answers about his nephew's case. I'm a Private Investigator and the deceased was a good friend of mine."

"Sorry, Mr. Redmon, but I can't discuss the case yet. I just got it this morning and I already have several opened cases on my desk. I promise I'll look at it as soon as I have time. Call me in a few days."

Before the detective could hang up, Jim blurted, "I thought you'd like to know that Andy Warren never was a heavy drinker and the accident happened in a part of the city that he never frequented. There are no close restaurants or bars nearby, and he was found in a neighborhood of apartment buildings and small specialty shops. Hardly a place to be completely inebriated and wandering out in the street."

The man was condescending, "And it wouldn't surprise me if he had been at a party at someone's apartment and out looking for a cab!"

"You're absolutely correct," agreed Jim. "It sure would make things easier if I could look at his phone. I think it would help."

The detective seemed to cool down at Jim's respectful reply. "I tell you what, Mr. Redmon, I'll look into his file this afternoon and let you know what I think. Gimme your number."

"For starters, call me Jim," and he gave him his number.

6.
Questions and Answers

When Jim woke on Tuesday morning, he thought, My list has suddenly shrunk; can't get into the apartment, no papers to look at, and no access to Andy's cell. Only one thing I can do: visit the site of the accident.

He knew businesses didn't open until ten so Jim waited, then took a cab to the location. He walked both sides of the street, noticing there were a few shops with *Open* signs displayed. He started with the small boutique first.

The shop seemed to have retro furnishings and vintage clothing. A saleslady greeted him.

"I wonder if I could ask you some questions about the hit-and-run accident that happened out front last week?"

The woman looked like she was in her mid-forties, but she was made up and dressed like a girl in her twenties. "Yes, I heard about it," she said. "I heard the man was drunk and someone hit him and left the scene."

"Were you in your shop when it happened?" he asked.

"No. I leave here at five every night and only heard about it the next day."

Jim smiled, said he appreciated it (as he handed her his card) and asked her to call him if she heard anything pertaining to the accident. The woman was all smiles and agreeable.

The next shop he visited was a smoke shop. He stepped in and was assailed with the pungent smell of cigars. The merchant was sitting on a stool behind the counter and engrossed in a TV show on his small set. He bellowed, "Can I help you?"

Jim went through the same routine he had with the last lady.

"I live upstairs over the shop, but never heard anything unusual. I was probably watching TV." He stopped and scratched his chin, "But you could ask the woman in the small bakery down the street. She lives above her shop too, and she might know something."

Down the block, Jim could smell the bakery shop before he saw the store front.

Barbara's Bakery was painted on the front window with pictures of various baked goods surrounding it. The *Open* sign was in plain view on the front door. When Jim entered, a bell rang and a woman entered from the back room carrying a tray.

"Hello! Come in and have a free sample of my delicious chocolate chip cookies...they just came out of the oven!"

"Actually, I wanted to ask you some questions about the hit-and-run accident that happened out front last week."

The woman smiled, and said, "You can still have a cookie and I'll be glad to answer any questions."

Jim reached out and helped himself to one. "I understand you live on the premises and wondered if you saw or heard anything the other night?" (He took a nibble and the cookie was delicious!)

"Yes, that's correct. I bake in the back and live upstairs over the shop. As far as seeing anything, I heard a car squeal around the corner and looked out the window to see what was happening. The car seemed to slow down for a brief stop, and when it sped up again, I could see a dark shape in the street. I honestly didn't know what happened but I did call the police because I thought they had hit a dog; never realizing it was a person. It's just awful!" she said with a shudder.

Jim felt like he had hit the jackpot. "I wonder if you could identify the car that was involved?"

"No, not really. As I said before, it was dark *and* not near any of the street lamps. But I do know that it was big, like a SUV or van."

"Could you think back and remember if you heard a car door slam?" asked Jim as he crossed his fingers.

The lady closed her eyes as she thought back to that dreadful night. "Yes, I DO remember hearing a car door slam! I guess the driver wanted to see what he hit."

Jim was elated that this woman was so observant. "I thank you so very much for your time. And those cookies are so good, I'd like to buy half a dozen!"

She was delighted and wrapped six chocolate chip cookies in a foil bag for him. After paying her, he gave her his card, thanked her, and left.

He thought, *Now what? I've got the rest of the day to fritter away until I meet Dave for dinner.* He decided to call Rebecca and find out if she could tell him how far it was to the shop Andy leased. After a short conversation, Jim hailed another cab.

The area of town was upscale and the place must have been a nice shop because it had a handsome wood door trimmed with brass fixtures. Jim tried to look through the store window, but he could see very little as someone had painted the window with a privacy paint. There was a small sign in the corner that said *FOR LEASE* and a number listed. Jim called the number and the phone was answered immediately.

"Hello, my name is Jim Redmon and I'm calling about the shop you have for lease." He supplied the address. "Could I make an appointment to see it?"

Jim responded, "I'm standing in front of the building now."

The man was surprised the For Lease sign was still in the window. "Well actually the shop won't be available for awhile. The man who leased it was killed in an accident recently and I'll have to check with my lawyer to see when it can go on the market again."

"I'm so sorry," said Jim." Could I still see the inside of the building?"

"I'm sure it would be okay. The gentleman didn't start renovations yet; however, he did have some things shipped there. But I don't believe it will keep you from looking at the space. Could I meet you there around two?

"Sounds good to me. I'll grab lunch in the meantime."

After the brief call, Jim decided to look for a place to have lunch. Down the street, he saw a little restaurant. After a light lunch, he decided to walk around the block to see if there was access to the back of the building. Finally, he saw an alley and walked toward the back of the shop. Sure enough, there was a small loading dock with a dumpster nearby. Most of the buildings were built close to the alley with nothing but an ordinary door. But the one Andy had was one with a drive that sloped down to a loading dock that received goods on ground level. It would be ideal for a person receiving furniture, and/or large items.

It was close to two when he turned the corner. Someone had just pulled up and parked in the loading zone. He stuck a sign in his car's window, and started for the shop. As he was about to put the key in the lock, Jim approached and offered his hand.

"I'm Jim Redmon and was told to be here at two o'clock to look at the building."

After the two men shook hands, the man introduced himself. "I'm Leo Cordisi and I'm the owner. Come in and have a look around."

When the two men entered, the owner turned on the lights. It was a large space with an old-world homey feel with hardwood floors and a handsome wood staircase in the rear. In his mind, this would be a great place to open an antique shop. Before Jim could get a word in, the owner started a hard-sell with him, spouting off the pluses, telling Jim the square footage and mentioning its great location. He then insisted they look at the entire place, including the basement; which he was proud to say was bone-dry. There was an ancient freight elevator that was still in service. "I also have a loading dock in the back, and a second floor for offices."

As the two men covered the space, Jim noticed a large opened crate. Behind it he saw a piece of furniture which looked like a desk. Cordisi said, "I think that's some of the stuff he had delivered here a few weeks ago. I don't think we should touch it." Jim nodded, noting several other boxes pushed against the wall.

Jim played the part of the interested party and asked how much. His jaw dropped when he heard the price. (It sure wasn't Chattanooga!) The two men bantered for another half hour and Jim had to admit the man knew he had a goldmine and was ready to get the place on the market again as soon as possible.

Making a move to leave, the owner asked him if he had a card and Jim started looking through pockets, making a show of not being able to find one. He had no intention of giving him his card.

"As soon as I've looked at a few other places, I'll call you if I'm interested. I'd really prefer to lease something available immediately, but I appreciate you taking the time to show your space to me; you have a great place!" Jim made a mental note to check Andy's keys to see if one of them belonged to this shop. He would really like to examine the bill of lading for the desk to see where it came from.

"The man I dealt with was interested in a lease/purchase option. Would you be interested in the same arrangement?" Cordisi asked.

Jim assured him he was only interested in leasing.

"I thought everything was settled until I read about the accident in the paper. I was shocked it was the same man I'd been doing business with."

"What kind of business was he going to put in?" inquired Jim.

"He was planning on opening an exclusive antique store. It would have been perfect for him; especially with that loading dock in back. So you'll understand why I can't lease it again until all this is settled."

The two swapped platitudes before saying their goodbyes.
By this time, it was late afternoon and Jim decided to go back to his hotel and have a cup of coffee, with the rest of his cookies.

7.
Antique Shops

Dave arrived at the restaurant before Jim. He was seated at the bar having a drink when his buddy entered. He quickly paid his bill and approached Jim. "This is a nice place. Have you been here before?" The two shook hands.

"No, but Andy frequented the place and Rebecca thought we'd enjoy it."

"She was right. Did you make a reservation?"

"Need you ask? I *have* been to New York before," Jim smugly retorted.

As the two were seated, Dave asked if he had made any headway on Andy's case. For the next several minutes, Jim filled him in on what he'd been doing all day.

"Sounds like you're at a standstill until you can get into the apartment or check out his cell and computer."

"You're right. The NYPD doesn't seem to be in a hurry to release any information. I wish I could get them to move on something before this whole case goes cold!" He shook his head with a disdainful smile, "I'm beginning to realize I'm an impatient dude."

Dave thoughtfully sipped his drink. "I'm only going to be in New York for another day or so, but if you think I can help, give me a call. I'm staying in the same hotel as you." The two friends enjoyed a pleasant meal and shared a cab back to their hotel. Jim was in bed by 10:30 p.m.

The following morning, Jim had some time to kill so he planned to check his computer for antique stores in New York. He decided to visit shops within a mile radius of his hotel, just to familiarize himself with antique stores. There were only three.

His first choice was located around five blocks away. It was a nice area removed from the city center and the store was around the corner from a neighborhood of brownstone walk-ups and apartments. It definitely wasn't a shop that imported expensive pieces.

The second shop was several streets away on a side street. Most of the buildings housed small businesses and eateries. As he approached, he noticed the location didn't seem nearly as good as the one Andy had leased. The proverbial bell rang when he opened the door.

"Good day," greeted the merchant.

"Hello!" replied Jim. "I wonder if you have time to educate me a little on imported antiques?"

"Sadly, I *do* have the time," the man quipped dryly. "But I don't know very much about imports as we carry very few of them. What is it you want to know?"

"I'm mainly interested in furniture pieces coming from England or France. I wondered if you could tell me anything about how the furniture gets into the U.S. and how it gets to the store?"

"I do know it is shipped from Europe in containers. Once they've arrived in the U.S., the containers are scanned for hidden or illegal contraband. They scan because I understand the authorities have learned the hard way there are many ways in which things can be concealed from the human eye."

"Am I right to assume that once they have passed inspection, the container is released and sent to the address on the shipping order?"

"I believe that is correct."

"Can you think of anything else?"

The merchant answered thoughtfully, "That's about all I know."

The next shop revealed about the same information. The proprietor suggested Jim find a gallery and ask them for information. He said they would probably be able to answer his questions better. He was grateful for some direction.

As Jim walked back to his hotel, he thought about some of the questions he planned to ask Rebecca over lunch.

When Jim got back to his room, he noticed he had a message from an unknown number. He quickly clicked *Call Back* and waited. Soon a man's voice answered, "Detective Stevens."

Jim sat down at the desk. "This is Jim Redmon, returning your call."

"Ah yes. I have some questions and answers for you, Mr. Redmon. Would it be possible for you to come by my office this afternoon?"

"Sure," responded Jim. "Would around three be satisfactory for you?"

"That'd be fine." Stevens gave him directions and ended the call.

As Jim was freshening up, his cell rang. It was Beth's cheerful voice, "Hi honey, how's it going?"

"Slow, but sure. When are you coming back to New York?"

"I'm leaving on Sunday afternoon, right after church. The Santiago's said they'll drive me to the airport. I'll take a cab to the hotel and should arrive around 4:30. Have you thought of anything else you want me to bring?"

"I'll call you after I find out what I need to get a gun permit." He paused thoughtfully, "Oh yes, bring both of our Passports." He didn't give her a chance to ask the question he knew she had on the tip of her tongue. He asked, "Have you talked to the kids?"

"Trey is on rotation and is enjoying it so much that he might change his mind about going into research!" She could imagine Jim's look of surprise. "And Emily, as expected, is enjoying her last year as a Tennessee Volunteer." She quietly added, "I'm sure you'll tell me when I see you why we may need our Passports."

If Beth even thinks we'll be going to Europe, she'll probably repack! Such a deal.

8.
Police Precinct

It was almost 2:30 pm when Jim headed over to Stevens' precinct. *Maybe I can get some information at the desk about carrying a gun in New York. Having to call all these cabs, I might as well kill two birds with one stone,* he thought.

Jim entered the building and it was like walking onto a set for a TV police drama.

The large desk was front and center with a huge police officer sitting behind it. He asked the officer where he could find out some information about getting a gun permit for New York.

"I'm a PI in a different state and I understand I *cannot possess a concealed weapon until I get a permit issued by local law enforcement,*" Jim recited.

"Yeah, I guess that's right. You have to go to the License Division with a completed application. Since you use it for your business, you'll need a recent utility bill, your original Social Security card, and Bureau of Security and Investigative Services (BSIS) permit also." Jim realized these were things he needed Beth to bring with her.

Jim got the address where he had to go and then told the man he had an appointment with Detective Stevens at three o'clock. The officer looked at his watch, "You're a little early, aren't you?"

"Thought I'd try to take care of the permit before I saw him."

"Well you can wait right over there and I'll tell him you're early." He motioned to a small seating area near the front door.

It wasn't long before Jim found himself shaking hands with the detective and was directed to a chair by his desk.

"I'm glad you could come in today, Mr. Redmon. Maybe we can clear up some of my questions, then you can ask me your questions afterward." Stevens had a yellow pad in front of him and picked up his pen. "How long did you know the deceased?"

"Since we were in Iraq together. We were in the same squad

and there are seven of us who've remained close. We were Andy's pall bearers."

"I was in Iraq but sad to say haven't kept in touch with anyone from back then." He made a note on his pad and continued. "Do you know much about Warren's business?"

"Not a lot. We don't talk much about business when we get together. But I do know that when he got out of the service, his childless uncle offered him a job. So he went to California and his uncle started teaching him about antiques and imports."

"What made him come to New York?"

"From what I understand, his uncle groomed him to develop business in Europe. Mr. Warren was mainly importing from Asia and could see the opportunity in England and France. I guess Andy became pretty successful and his uncle made him a partner after only a year. Andy said it was smarter and more reasonable to be based in New York for European goods and his uncle agreed."

"Have you ever visited your friend here in New York?"

Jim thought that was a strange question. "No, I haven't. He invited me and my wife to come up, but we never made it."

"Do you know if he had an office here?"

"I believe he worked out of his apartment. He had a second bedroom that, from what I observed, he had turned into an office."

"I thought you said you never visited him in New York?" Stevens shot back.

Jim calmly answered. "That's right. My wife and I had lunch with Andy's uncle the day after the funeral. When he asked us to come back to the apartment with him, we saw it had been ransacked. As I looked around, I noticed the desk, file cabinet and office paraphernalia in a spare room. I just figured it was his office."

The detective tipped back in his chair. "I see here that you're a Private Investigator in Chattanooga, Tennessee. How long you been doing that?"

"I went to law school and had my own practice for several years but got bored and decided to open my own investigative services business. It was a good move and I'm not sorry I changed directions."

"I hope you don't mind, Mr. Redmon, but I did a little background check on you before you came in. I understand a few years ago your son got into a little trouble and your "squad" and you managed to solve the problem. I guess you and your buddies *are* pretty tight."

Jim was shocked the man had been able to access that

information. "Actually, we cleared up two problems; my father had been murdered when I was in high school and the case had never been solved. Ironically, we were able to solve that one, too."

Stevens changed his mind about the man sitting in front of him. *He isn't the hick I figured he'd be,* he thought. *In fact, I'd guess he's pretty sharp and from what I hear, his friends aren't slouches either!*

"Do you have any idea who would want to kill Andrew Warren?" he asked.

"No, but his uncle has hired me to try to find out, and I intend to do just that. It's one of the reasons I'm so anxious to get into his apartment, check his computer, and also get his cell back. I'm at a standstill until those things are released to me."

"Give us a couple more days and we'll allow you access to the apartment."

Jim enlightened the man, "Actually, Mr. Warren has offered to let my wife and I stay in Andy's apartment while I'm working on the case. We'd like to move over there as soon as possible."

"I bet. Those hotel bills will eat you up," the officer muttered.

Jim held his tongue and didn't comment. The hotel bill would *not* be a problem but he felt Stevens had no need to know about his financial status.

The detective picked up his phone and asked for the Property desk. He asked them to have Andrew Warren's personal effects ready; he'd be down to pick them up shortly.

Jim stated, "Now it's time for *my* questions. Have any witnesses to the accident come forward?"

Stevens smiled, "None, yet. And considering the hour of the evening when it occurred, we don't expect any."

"Did you talk to any of the people in the neighborhood?"

"Like I said, it was late and all the shops were closed."

Jim was surprised. He knew the NYPD were sharp investigators and was perplexed by Stevens' answer. It was Investigation 101 and for some reason the guy wasn't forthcoming.

"Could you tell me where they took Andy? The account says he died in the ambulance on the way; at least that's what they told his uncle."

The detective was surprised Redmon asked the question. "Why is that important?" he replied impatiently.

"Anybody I can talk to regarding the night he was killed will help me." Jim paused, "Sort of like some of the questions you asked *me*!" He grinned. "It helps a person to round out the whole picture."

Stevens frostily replied. "Well, if that's all, Mr. Redmon, let's go down to Property and get Mr. Warren's personal effects." He stood up.

"Actually, Detective Stevens, I'd like the name of the hospital before we leave." Stevens wrote the address on a paper and handed it to Jim. The two then left and took the elevator down to the basement.

Jim signed for Andy's things and opened the envelop at the desk. The cell wasn't there; nor were there any keys. He caught Stevens before he got on the elevator. "Andy's cell and keys are missing. Can you clear this up for me?"

Stevens looked shocked. "What do you mean, they're missing? Everything they collected from the body should be in there!" He was aggravated and grabbed the envelope, reading the contents. "I guess there wasn't a cell on him, nor any keys, because they aren't listed here," he said with finality.

Now it was Jim's turn to be shocked. "His uncle specifically said he was sure the police had his cell...because Andy never went anywhere without it. And I can't imagine a person going out without his apartment key. I was with the police when they went through the apartment after it was ransacked. They found no phone." He walked back to the counter, pulled out his own cell and called Andy's number. A very faint ring was heard.

Jim looked at Stevens and asked him to go in the cage and find the ringing phone.

The detective looked uncomfortable, but went into the cage and found the phone in the back, on a small desk hooked up to a charger. Stevens glanced at the man working the desk as if asking a question, *what the hell is going on here?*

Jim asked, "Does the NYPD often get this sloppy?" Not expecting an answer, he continued. "And I don't really think they expected to get called on this because there is no mention of his cell phone or keys on this Contents list!" Jim was hot and Stevens knew it.

Stevens blustered, "I don't know what this is all about but I assure you, I'm going to get to the bottom of it!"

Jim reached out his hand, "I'll take the cell phone if you don't mind." The cell was reluctantly handed over and Jim slipped it into the envelope. "I'll call you in a couple of days to get approval to enter Andy's apartment."

As Jim left, he was stewing. A Bible verse from Proverbs popped into his head. Beth was always quoting pertinent scriptures to him and this verse was a zinger: "He who is slow to anger is better than the mighty, and he who rules his spirit is mightier than he who rules the city." Jim could have replied scathingly to Stevens; he was glad he didn't. He'd have to remember to tell Beth what a good boy he had been.

9.
Shipping

While Jim was with Detective Stevens, Paul Masters had beeped in. Jim decided to call him back after he left the precinct. When he was settled in a cab, he returned Paul's call.

"Hey Paul. Sorry I didn't pick up, but I was talking with the detective in charge of Andy's case."

"I just heard from my friend who moved to New York. He *is* with the NYPD. He's been doing some digging around for me and guess what he said? And I quote: 'There's something fishy going on about this case. They've put a lid on it so tight that not even fumes can escape!' My buddy talked with a good friend from the precinct handling Andy's case and he said it'd be better if we backed off. What's going *on*?"

Jim told him he didn't know. "Can you believe they typed up a new Content list at the Property desk, leaving the cell phone off so they wouldn't have to hand it over?" He told Paul how he discovered Andy's phone.

"The way I figure it, somebody on the inside is in cahoots with whomever is messin' with this case. When they find out I have Andy's phone, somebody's head is going to roll. Lucky for me, they didn't turn the thing off but it rang loud and clear. It was charged and I think someone was in the process of, or about to check it out."

Jim continued. "I'm going downtown to the hospital where they took Andy and pronounced him DOA. Maybe I can catch a break."

Paul stated, "Sounds to me like you already got one when you discovered that cell phone."

"I wish Butch were here so he could check this cell out."

Paul was thoughtful, then suggested, "Why don't you overnight it to him? Call him first, explain what you're up against, and ask him if you could send it. If he says yes, you can ask him to overnight it back."

Jim agreed it was a great idea. He called Butch and found him at work.

"Hey buddy. You said you'd be glad to help out if I needed anything. So here's what has happened." And Jim supplied the details. "Needless to say, I need it done right away and need for you to Fed-Ex it back. Can you do that for me?"

"More than happy to, Captain. Give me the hotel's address. Luckily I have no projects I'm working on right at the moment."

Jim was more than pleased. On the way back to his hotel, he asked the cabbie if he knew of a Fed-Ex office on the way. The cabbie took him directly to the store.

David Weintroub was about to finish up a written report when his cell rang. He saw the caller was the captain. "Hey Jim. What's up?"

Once again, Jim went through Andy's cell phone saga. He paused and asked, "Is there any way I can find out who's calling the shots on this?"

Dave replied, "I don't get information from other agencies *willingly* handed to me. I'm sure you've heard of the competition. But I do know someone over at the FBI; I might be able to find out something."

"How about I meet you in the hotel dining room and I buy you dinner? Then we can discuss everything?" asked Jim.

"If you think I'd turn down *another* free meal in New York, you're crazy. Would seven-thirty be okay? I have to finish this report."

"I'll see you in the lobby at seven-thirty." After he hung up, Jim got his list out and crossed off several points and added some more.

When Dave and Jim arrived at the restaurant, they were ushered to a table in the corner. Even though Jim hadn't requested one, he was glad their table was out of the mainstream. *I guess I'll always be paranoid about eavesdroppers,* he thought.

They talked about Andy's case and Jim relayed his conversation with Detective Stevens. "I don't lose my temper often, but today I came close."

Dave shared about a phone call he'd had after talking with Jim earlier. "It was my source at the FBI who agreed to do some snooping for me. He was surprised at how tight this case was nailed down. He said you'd think they were protecting national secrets! He finally found out from a secretary that there did seem to be a connection to the FBI on this one. She couldn't find out anything other than that." Dave took a swig of his beer. "If the FBI is in on it, I should be able to find out something myself. I'll start turning over rocks tomorrow and I'll call you with any results."

Their food came and the subjects discussed were sports, politics, and the weather.

After the two friends parted, Jim thought to himself, *No time like the present. Better chance of finding the same hospital personnel on tonight's rotation rather than tomorrow.* He leaned forward and asked the cabbie to take him to Bellevue Hospital. As the cab neared the hospital, he asked the driver to drop him at the Emergency entrance. Jim knew he'd probably be here awhile because it was Friday night. He approached the desk and asked, "Is there any way I could talk to the medical personnel that was on duty the night they brought in Andrew Warren after a hit-and-run accident last week?" The girl looked blankly at him.

"Let me rephrase that," Jim said with humor. "Last week there was a hit-and-run victim brought into your ER. . .his name was Andrew Warren. . .I need to talk with the medical personnel that treated him. . .Would that be possible?"

The girl typed the name in her computer and after several minutes stated, "There's only one nurse on duty tonight that was here that evening. She's busy with a patient now but I'll let her know you're here. By the way, are you with the police?"

"No, I'm not. I'm a Private Investigator who was hired by the family to investigate the situation. They suspect foul play."

The receptionist found that intriguing and supplied Jim with the name of the nurse *and* the doctor that was on the floor when Andrew was brought in.

"I thank you so much for your help," he said, dazzling her with a smile. He found a seat and picked up a sports magazine to read while he waited.

After about thirty minutes, a nurse approached him and introduced herself, "If you'll follow me, I think we can discuss this privately in another room."

Looking at his surroundings, Jim figured the small room was probably used for doctors to talk with family members. He opened a small notebook and took out his pen. "If you don't mind, I'd like to ask you some questions. Andrew Warren's family has hired me to look into his death by a hit-and-run driver last week." He looked up at the nurse and saw her look of surprise.

"What is it?" he asked.

"Well, you surprised me by referring to him as being dead. I know that he was alive when he was brought in, and they whisked him away to OR. He was seriously injured but alive."

Jim was astonished, but quickly recovered. "No. The police indicated he was dead on arrival, but maybe the person who I talked to *assumed* that." He paused, thinking fast.

"Are there records kept of people who have died in this hospital?"

"Why yes, there is. You can call the Department of Death Certificates, or Medical Records. Of course, those offices are closed after five."

"When the receptionist gave me your name, she also mentioned a Dr. Hajadi. Would he happen to be on the floor tonight?"

"No, I'm sorry he isn't." She added, "Funny thing, but Dr. Hajadi went off duty right after Mr. Warren was brought in. I hear he was leaving early to go on vacation and had to leave the hospital that evening. It was strange."

Jim inquired, "What do you mean, 'strange'?"

"Well, he had many patients in cubicles still waiting to be examined, and there was no mention he would be leaving early. Plus he had told me that he and his wife were looking forward to going on vacation to India in April. They were going for a big family wedding." She shrugged her shoulders. "Go figure." She seemed to dismiss it. "Is that all, Mr. Redmon?"

"Yes, and thanks for taking the time to talk with me." The nurse left the room and Jim followed her out.

The exhausted Private Investigator returned to his hotel room. He had scarcely enough energy to take his clothes off before he fell into bed.

10.
Appointments

On Thursday morning, Jim decided to try to find the ambulance service that answered the call that took Andy to the hospital. He started calling and hit the jackpot on the second number.

"Yes sir. For the night in question I see where one of our crews picked up a hit-and-run victim in the area which you mentioned."

Jim asked how he would go about getting an appointment to talk with the paramedics that took the call. He could tell she thought it was a strange request by the way she answered. He added, "I'm a Private Investigator and have been hired to rule out foul play regarding this hit-and-run. It really would be helpful if I could talk to the crew that took the victim to the hospital."

The woman was helpful and suggested Jim come by their place of business the next morning. She cautioned there may be a chance the No. 43 guys would be out on a call. Jim assured her he understood but would be there at 9:30 a.m.; he asked her to tell the crew that he would be coming.

He felt good that it was done. He had a plan and things to do tomorrow. He sure wished he didn't have to call a taxi every time he went some place!

Hustling down to the front of his hotel, Jim caught a cab to the restaurant where he was supposed to meet Rebecca. He had decided to arrive a little earlier than they agreed, as he wanted to check out the place and observe her arrival. Obviously they knew her because when Rebecca walked through the door, the host greeted her like a long-lost friend. The two spoke quietly for a few moments, and Jim noticed the concerned expression on the man's face; he obviously had heard about Andy. Rebecca posed a question, and the host nodded, leading her toward Jim's banquette.

The admiring glances were hard to miss as Rebecca regally followed the host across the restaurant to where he sat. He arose to greet her, and she smiled as she slid around onto the bench next to him. The host supplied menus and the two made small talk as they waited for the waitress to come and take their drink orders.

As they looked at the menu, Jim inquired, "Any suggestions what I should order for lunch?"

"Actually, I can wholeheartedly recommend anything you choose. The food is delicious!"

He nodded, and chose a robust Reuben sandwich with the restaurant's specialty fries on the side. Rebecca had a nice salmon salad with crackers on the side. *I guess that's one of the reasons she's in such great shape and I'm fighting to keep this tire off,* he thought.

Jim waited until after their lunch was served before he started quizzing her. "Rebecca, Beth said you had noticed Andy was having a problem sleeping about two months ago. Did he seem preoccupied? I ask because that was around the same time he called me. He never seemed to get around to telling me why he really called and I definitely assumed he had changed his mind about divulging whatever he was going to say."

"He was clearly troubled about something," Rebecca declared. "I told Beth he never confided in me, much to my regret." Her eyes welled up and she became silent. Jim held his tongue until the moment passed; he could see her emotions were raw. She continued, "I guess he still wasn't sure he could trust me."

"There's one thing about Andy; he didn't share easily with anyone! I don't think it had anything to do with you, Rebecca. From what his uncle said, he surmised Andrew was closer to making a firm commitment to you than any other woman he'd ever dated."

She was surprised. "I wish he'd said something to me! I felt closed out so many times and it was getting harder and harder to be on the outside. In fact, I was close to ending our relationship because I was so desperately in love with him and figured he was *not* in love with me enough to make a commitment." She looked down at her hands folded in her lap. When she looked up, her green eyes were glazed with tears.

Jim forged ahead. "Can you remember when his demeanor changed and the sleeplessness started?"

"Come to think of it, it was around the time that Andy started looking into leasing his own space. Oddly, he asked me not to mention it to anyone."

"Can you give me a list of his friends?" Rebecca nodded. Jim added, "Andy never talked to me about his friends or activities. Come to think of it, none of us did when we were at our reunions.

"You know, Rebecca, I don't know much about the antique business. I know Andy mentioned that once when he went to Europe, he usually purchased for shopkeepers and an occasional customer. But I have a question: When they arrived, where were the items sent?"

"If it wasn't sent directly to a customer, Andy had a friend that allowed him to put items in his small gallery on consignment. It worked out for both of them but it didn't happen often. Andy knew his customers very well and vice versa. When they saw he had excellent decorating taste, they tried to hire him. He wasn't interested in getting roped into that part of the business. When he realized I had some experience in decorating, he started asking my opinion. As time went on, he asked for advice more and more, which thrilled me. He jokingly asked if I would be interested in a permanent position as a decorator when he opened his own shop. I asked if he was serious, but he just laughed." Rebecca showed a touch of resentment as she added, "He couldn't even commit to *that*!"

"Could you use the income, Rebecca?"

"Not really. I received a sizeable settlement from my divorce. With wise investing, I'll be okay." She paused a moment, "But it would be nice to find something to do that I enjoy, and I *enjoy* decorating."

Jim looked with renewed interest at this lovely woman. As far as he was concerned, Andy was a dunce for taking her for granted.

"Rebecca, has Andy been carrying a gun very long?"

She thought back and remembered about the time she first noticed it. "We had gone back to his apartment one evening and he slipped off his jacket. I reached to hang it up and felt the weight of a gun in his pocket. I guess he noticed my alarm and quickly said, 'I realized I needed protection when I carry large amounts of cash on me. I guess I forgot the gun was in my pocket.' It was lame and I said so. He didn't want to talk about it and it was never mentioned again. This happened before the scenario I related at the funeral."

"Did Andy stay at the same places when he went to London or Paris?"

"He did when he could. They weren't fancy, high-priced hotels; just small establishments that catered to businessmen. He would often make the hotel his base and rent a car to go different places. He promised to take me along on one of his trips and I was excited." She looked into space. "It'll never happen now."

"Can you remember the names of the places he went?"

"No, but I can tell you where you can get that information. Andy always kept good records and he has a folder in his desk that contains all his traveling receipts. It should be in there. He also kept a journal of sorts highlighting his appointments."

"Sounds like Andy. Do you think there would be anywhere in his records where he kept the names of business contacts over there? I'd like to call some of them."

"You can try his rolodex on top of his desk."

"I'd really like to talk with the guy who owns the gallery that had the arrangement with Andy. Do you know his name"

"You can also find his number in the rolodex. The man's name is Fred Houseman but I don't recall the name of his gallery."

"I'm waiting on the NYPD to tell me when I can enter Andy's apartment. There's so much I want to investigate and it's very frustrating to have to wait."

In the course of their conversation, Jim asked Rebecca where she lived. She told him her apartment overlooked Central Park, and supplied the address. He was shocked because he was sure the building's condos sold for well over a million. *I guess she did get a nice settlement,* he thought.

After Jim paid the bill, the two parted and got into their respective cabs.

11.
Hospital Mystery

Friday morning Jim readied himself to keep his appointment at the ambulance office. He decided to call first, and save himself a trip if the crew was out.

He responded, "This is Jim Redmon. I came in yesterday hoping to talk with the Paramedics that took a hit-and-run victim to Bellevue last week."

The girl wasn't nearly as friendly as the day before. She said she remembered their conversation, but said, "I'm sorry, but that crew is out right now. I don't know when they'll be back so I can't help you."

Jim asked, "Could you tell me when they *will* be in?" She said she didn't know. When he asked for their names, she said it was against company policy to give out that information, plus she was sorry she had to hang up because she had another call coming in.

Jim found himself about to speak into a dead phone and knew he had been deftly stonewalled.

It was nearing ten o'clock when Jim called Philip Warren. The gentleman answered his phone promptly. Jim apologized if it was too early.

"No, no, not at all. I'm always an early riser." He paused. "Have you called with any news for me, Jim?"

"This case becomes more and more puzzling. The police gave me an envelope holding Andy's personal effects and there was no cell phone. When I challenged them, they said there was no cell phone found on his body. I immediately called Andy's number, and I heard a phone ringing back in the property cage! When they retrieved it, they had egg on their faces.

"Last night, I went to the hospital hoping to find someone on the floor that was there the night they brought Andy in. Luckily, the nurse was, but the doctor mysteriously has taken a vacation starting the night Andy was brought in! As you might well imagine, I'm beginning to think this wasn't some random hit-and-run. My curiosity is really peaked and I can tell you I'm determined to find out what's going on."

"Good, Jim. I haven't been satisfied with anything I've heard so far. And I can tell, you aren't either."

"While I've got you on the phone, Philip, would you call the police department tomorrow and ask them to release Andy's apartment and his computer. Ironically, there were no keys on Andy when they took him to Bellevue. If you have an extra key to his apartment, I'd appreciate it if you'd overnight it to me here at the hotel. I'll feel a whole lot better when I can start combing through his things."

"I'll send the key and call the police department this afternoon! And I hope the next time we talk, some of these *mysteries* will be solved."

The next call was to Rebecca. He left a message on her machine. He told her he needed that list of Andy's friends and their numbers. She called back within ten minutes.

"It's Rebecca, Jim. I was on the phone and couldn't get off. Sorry. What can I do for you?"

"As I said in my message, I sure would appreciate it if you could compile a list of Andy's good friends and their numbers."

"Sure. I completely forgot that you asked me. I have to go by your hotel tomorrow morning and I'll drop off what I have at the desk."

After thanking Rebecca, Jim hung up and decided to take it easy the rest of the day. *Yesterday I did enough work for TWO days!*

Jim went into the bathroom and noticed his shaving kit had been moved. He erased the thought from his mind assuming it was the maid. As he opened the dresser drawer to get something, he noticed that things had been moved. Not many people would notice, but Jim was a neat-freak. He sat down on the bed. *Someone has carefully gone through my things,* he thought. The next thing he did was check for bugs; including his luggage. He didn't find anything, but made a decision to be very careful about any information he shared or left in his room.

It was a great book and he was enjoying every word; one of those you could hardly put down. He read, *"The man was wondering if he could shoot his way out...",* and his cell rang.

"Can't get a moment's peace!" Jim hustled over to the desk and snatched up the hotel phone. "Hello," he retorted.

"So sorry to disturb you, Mr. Redmon, but a package arrived from Washington, DC for you and you will have to sign for it. Could you come down?" the man asked cautiously.

"Sorry for my rudeness," he apologized. "I'll be right down."

When Jim brought the package upstairs, he was pleasantly surprised when he saw it was Andy's cell phone including a typewritten report from Butch. It looked like Butch had worked on it as soon as he got it, immediately typed up his findings, and sent it back.

It dawned on Jim that this phone may be what the thief was looking for in his room. *Could it be Stevens,* he thought, *I'm sure it never dawned on him that I would have dropped the cell in the mail on my way home from the precinct!*

The report stated that he had gone back a couple months and only included some of the questionable people Andy had talked with. There was a man named Lockman that seemed friendly at first, but by the time Butch had gone through week's of messages, Lockman had become threatening. He was irritated, saying he wanted the goods right away and he'd do what he had to in order to get what belonged to him. He ended the conversation by hanging up without a goodbye. (Butch couldn't trace the number as it was a burner phone.)

Goods? What belonged to him? Jim was perplexed. *He had to get into Andy's apartment and check the rolodex to see who this guy was.*

The next call was to someone Andy called Foster. Andy told Foster that he'd had a call from Lockman and the guy wasn't happy. Andy asked, "What should I do? You've got his stuff."

Talk about a mystery, Jim's brain was working overtime. *I'll check Rebecca's list when I get it. I need to find out who Lockman and Foster are.*

12.
Who's Who

The next morning, the front desk said a letter had arrived for him. When Jim got on the elevator, he scanned the names on Rebecca's list. Glancing down the list, he saw there was a gallery named Houseman Galleries with only a number listed. There was no one by the name of Foster.

Jim called the gallery first. A receptionist said Mr. Houseman was out and wouldn't be back until late afternoon. Instead of leaving his name, he told her he'd call back.

Going down the list, the first name was Michael Pagrino. He called, but Pagrino was out.

The next man was George Walters and said he'd be glad to meet Jim for coffee. As soon as Jim got in a cab, he decided to call Dave, who was leaving New York that afternoon. He told him about Rebecca's list and relayed what he'd been doing. Dave said he'd call periodically to check on his progress. In the meantime, he'd continue to see what he could find out about the FBI's involvement.

"While I've got you on the phone, Dave, I was wondering if you knew of someone I could hire to drive for me? This calling cabs for every little thing is a pain!"

"Let me make some calls and I'll call you right back."

"Great! I'm meeting one of Andy's friends for coffee. Call me in about an hour."

The coffee shop was full and as soon as a table became available, he walked over and claimed it. Shortly afterward, a man came in looking around and Jim stood, motioning him over. "Are you George Walters?" he asked.

"Yes. I recognize you from the funeral." The two men shook hands and George asked, "Have you ordered yet?"

"No, I just got the table." No sooner had Walters sat down, the waitress came over and they both ordered coffee.

Walters smiled, saying, "So you're the famous captain Andy

spoke of so highly!"

Jim replied with a laugh, "I don't know whether you'd call me famous, but we did serve together in Iraq. I appreciate you taking the time to meet me; Andy's uncle hired me to look into Andy's death. I'm a PI and would appreciate any help I can get." He paused, "Were you and Andy friends for long?"

"Oh yeah. We used to take in a ballgame occasionally. And when the mood hit us, we used to go out lookin' for women," he added jokingly.

"Had you seen him recently?"

"Not as much as I used to. As I'm sure you know, Andy and Rebecca Langley had become quite an item. We used to double-date occasionally and I could see the writing on the wall."

"And what was that?" asked Jim.

"They were crazy about one another. I'd never seen Andy act like that around a woman before, so I knew it was serious."

Jim nodded his head, not offering any comment.

"I knew he was a successful antique dealer and went to Europe several times a year to buy some treasures."

"How did he get customers?"

"I think mostly by word-of-mouth. I understand he had quite an extensive customer base and word spread about his talents. I guess that's what happens if you're a good salesman."

"Where were his *treasures* delivered?"

"I understand just within the last year he developed an understanding with the owner of a gallery uptown. I believe the name is Houseman Galleries."

There's that name again, thought Jim. He asked, "Do you know what Andy's arrangements were with the gallery?"

"I think Andy told me he had been there with customers several times and he and the owner got to talking. One thing led to another, and Houseman agreed to allow Andy to have some of his antiques delivered to his gallery in return for Andy making some purchases for him in Europe. The arrangement served both men well but Andy never told me if he had anything delivered at the galleries since."

"Do you know anything about Mr. Houseman?

"He has an excellent gallery and reputation. He carries higher-end antiques and Andy's keen eye for purchasing priceless items fit right in with Houseman's high quality taste. Naturally, Houseman and Andy worked out a reasonable arrangement for both of them. Andy didn't have everything sent to the gallery; there were many that were shipped directly to the customer." He sipped his coffee.

"Not too long ago, Andy mentioned he had just signed a lease for his own shop. He made arrangements with the landlord to have a few items sent there before they finalized the deal. I guess Andy trusted him."

"Do you know if Houseman came to Andy's funeral?" Jim inquired.

"I've never seen him, so I wouldn't know if he was there."

"Would you say they were friends outside of business?"

"I think it was strictly business."

The two men finished their coffee and shared some small talk before they left.

Jim talked with several more people on Rebecca's list. None offered as much information as Walters. Jim had an uncanny ability to sense when he should wait, back off, or plow on. As regarding the Houseman Galleries, he decided to wait. His gut told him it wasn't the right time to make it known that Philip Warren had hired him.

Another man on the list was a realtor friend. He knew Andy was serious about leasing his own space but he never got back with him so he assumed the decision was off the table. *Obviously he didn't know Andy had already leased a place,* thought Jim.

Dave called and had some incredible news. He had a friend who retired early from the NYPD. He was bored out of his mind and would jump at the chance to have a job driving for Jim. Dave gave him the phone number, saying, "He's expecting a call and I'll let you two go from there. His name is Manny Randolf. Let me know what happens; I think he'll be a great asset."

Jim called him immediately. "Manny? This is Jim Redmon, Dave Weintroub's friend. He told me to call you about a job driving for me while I'm in New York."

"Yeah, we just hung up! Thanks for calling me."

"Could you come by my hotel this afternoon so we can talk face to face?"

"Sure. What's the address?"

The two completed their plans and Jim prepared to interview the man he hoped to hire to drive him around this huge city.

Around 4:30, Jim opened the door to the biggest man he had come face to face with for a long time. He was even bigger than Jerry. He was at least six foot five, and built like a linebacker. His head was bald, and he was impeccably dressed.

"Hey Manny. Come in, come in. I'm Jim Redmon!" The two

shook hands and Jim winced at the man's grip. He led the *giant* into the sitting area. For the next hour, Jim asked questions and found himself telling Manny about his being hired by Philip Warren, the mystery surrounding the case, the kind of chauffeuring he contemplated, and where he was from.

Manny grinned. "So a southern boy, eh? My mama's people come from Alabama. We went down there one summer and I was never so hot in my life! I decided then and there I'd go to a beach in Florida if I ever wanted to get cooked!"

Jim laughed. "If you don't mind my saying so Manny, you don't look old enough to be retired!"

"I retired early. I got caught up in a situation and decided to get out. Financially it wasn't the best time to retire because shortly afterward my wife got cancer. She died eight months later and I was *glad* I could be home with her. Then my boy up and joined the Marines. Sure is lonely around my house."

"Sorry to hear about your wife. What are you doing now?"

"Early on, me and my wife each bought a life insurance policy. I actually thought she'd be spending mine and not the other way around. With part of the money, I paid cash for a small condo in a modest neighborhood. It's a roof over my head and its far better than the neighborhood where I grew up. I put what was left over in a safe deposit box. I might want to travel someday. My small pension allows me enough to pay bills. It isn't much, but I'm pretty content." The big man looked at Jim, "You got a family?"

"Yes. A wife and two grown kids. My son is in medical school at Emory and my daughter is in her senior year at the University of Tennessee. My wife is joining me here on Sunday. She went back home after Andy's funeral and is picking up some things for us while we're in New York. By the way, we'll probably be staying at my deceased friend's apartment instead of here. I'm just waiting for the police to release it to me."

"Who's leading the investigation? I may know him."

"A Detective Stevens. I haven't figured him out yet. I do know one thing, he has a short fuse and isn't very friendly."

Manny laughed out loud. "You can say that again, but a better cop you won't find. He's been in the department since he got out of high school. He decided to get his college education at night school, got his diploma and, wallah, he rose in the system. He's honest and well-respected.

"I worked out of the same precinct but he's in Homicide. To put your mind at rest, Stevens leaves no stone unturned. He doesn't like coincidences and handles each case as if it were his own family. I think you're in good hands."

"Well Manny, I think you'll be a great driver for me. Since you don't have any other responsibilities, it sounds like you'll be able to come at my beck and call. *That* I need."

The two men began discussing Manny's salary and Jim's expectations.

"Can you start right away?" Jim asked.

The big man beamed. "I sure can. If you don't mind, I'd like you to introduce me to the manager. They usually have a garage or parking area a driver can use. It makes it all much easier if I arrive early or need to park for an extended time."

Jim thought, *"I can't believe I lucked out so good. And I sure don't mind him watching my back."*

"Let's go down and see the manager and then we'll go have dinner; on me of course. . .and you'll drive." Jim laughed.

As the two sat over dinner, they got better acquainted. He formed the opinion that Manny was trustworthy and would be a valuable driver. The two men made arrangements to meet for breakfast in the hotel early Monday morning.

That evening when he got back to his room, Jim decided to call Beth. Yes, she had picked up all the items on his list. No, he didn't want to talk about the Passports. Yes, he did talk with Dave about a driver and had hired one, and, yes, he couldn't wait to see her. After Beth hung up, she thought, *that man wouldn't know what a friendly conversation was if it rose up and bit him. He states his business and hangs up.* Totally frustrated, she just shook her head.

Sunday morning, the Concierge called him over to give him an envelope from Philip Warren. *Ah, the key!* When Jim reached Warren, he found out the apartment would be available for he and Beth on Monday. He was pleased. After breakfast, he went up to his room and decided to read. When he woke an hour later, he was shocked he had drifted off to sleep. *I guess I'm more tired than I thought,* he realized. So much for the book. He called room service for lunch and watched sports all afternoon. The afternoon wore on and Jim checked the time and realized Beth would arrive soon. He decided to go down and wait in the lobby.

Beth walked through the main entrance and beamed when she saw her husband waiting for her. Her heart always did a little skip when she saw him after a time of separation. She considered how very handsome her man was. He smiled, revealing the dimple in his right cheek. As his piercing eyes swept over her, she knew he was as glad to see her as she was to see him.

Jim's thoughts were just as admiring: *She is so fine!*

13.
Detective Detecting

On Monday, Detective Robert Stevens got in early and didn't clock in until he had a chance to check personnel. He got on his computer and advanced to Property, bringing up the rotation schedule.

Joe Diago was on the desk from 7:30 a.m. to 4:30 p.m. Eric Jones relieved him, working until ll:30. The next shift fell to the new guy, Ralph Mercer.

Stevens started to investigate each man. He found Diago had been in Property for nine years and was looking to retire in a couple years. He'd been on Patrol before then and had a nondescript record.

Eric Jones was a go-getter. He'd risen quickly and had made some good arrests while on the street. He was 29 years old and had been on the Property desk about a year. Stevens could read the writing on the wall that this kid was going to try to take the next step into the Evidence Control Unit and eventually transfer into the Crime Scene Unit. He had his work cut out for him, for over a hundred men were vying for one or two slots in Crime Scene.

Ralph Mercer didn't have much of a record; he'd been on the desk about six months. In fact, Stevens thought he needed to scope this guy out himself. He decided to go down and talk with Jones just after the man clocked in for his shift.

The elevator opened and Stevens saw a young man with a neat appearance. He approached the desk and said, "I'm Detective Stevens. I don't think we've met."

The guy stood and held out his hand, "I'm Eric Jones. I haven't seen you down here before, detective."

"No. I don't get down here much. I'm checking on something that's related to one of my cases. Hope you can help me."

"Yeah. I heard about the cell phone that got misplaced earlier. I never saw it."

"Did you see anyone messin' around who shouldn't have been in Property yesterday?"

"No. The only people I see are those bringing things in before they're transferred to the Property Clerk Division. I didn't receive the vic's belongings the night he was run down. That must have been Mercer; he works the graveyard shift."

"Thanks for the info," said Stevens. "I'm trying to figure out why the phone wasn't included with his things. Do you recall ever seeing the envelope holding his stuff?"

"I saw it but didn't read it. It was just one of many envelopes in the Property crawer."

"Well thanks, anyway," said Stevens as he turned for the elevator. He turned back as if he forgot something. "Hey. Can you fill me in about Mercer? I'll be gone by the time he reports for duty."

Jones was contemplative seeming to determine how much he should say. "Well, I really don't have much time to connect with him as I'm going off duty when he comes on."

"Does he get in on time?" asked Stevens.

"Most of the time. A couple of times he called me to tell me he'd be a little late and asked me not to mention it to anyone, so naturally he was friendly when he came in."

"I take it he isn't friendly all the time?"

"Look, I don't want to get anyone in trouble, but he's *different*. I can't put my finger on anything but he isn't like most of the guys I know on the force."

"Has he made any friends here, that you know of?"

Jones thought before he spoke. "Yeah, a guy who just started at the precinct; he's on patrol now and I've seen him with Mercer when he comes in. The two look pretty tight and whisper a lot. I don't know his name."

"Okay, Jones. Thanks for being so up-front with me. It helps me form a picture of him." With that, the detective turned and got on the elevator adding, "Would you leave a message for Mercer to call me?" The young man said he would be glad to do so.

That morning, when Jim entered the breakfast room, Manny was already having a cup of coffee, reading the paper. He looked up with his wide smile as Jim strode over to join him.

"Anything interesting going on in the big apple this morning?" he said, pointing to the newspaper.

"Just the usual news: murder, scandal, and robberies, to name a few."

Jim chuckled. Getting down to business, he said, "Around ten, I'd like to go take a look at the Houseman Galleries. I don't think Mr.

Houseman will be in that early, which is okay with me as I'd like to freely wander."

"I'll be waiting out front at ten."

"I intend to check with Mr. Warren to see if he called the precinct to get Andy's apartment released to me. If it's ready, tomorrow I'll need you to take me over there."

"I'll be ready when you are."

Jim looked at him, and with a smile said, "You wouldn't be interested in moving to Chattanooga, would you?" They both laughed.

"I'm going to go up and make some phone calls. Do you want to hang out here until I'm ready?"

"Nah. I'll wait in my car. After I finish the paper, I'll go down and read a book. Just call me if you need me sooner."

Jim asked Manny to drive them someplace for dinner. "I'm looking forward to you meeting Beth when you pick us up. "My wife got in yesterday afternoon."

Manny said he'd be ready when Jim called. "Would you like me to suggest a place?" Jim was more than agreeable.

When he got back to the room, Beth was just coming into the sitting room. After a morning kiss, Jim sat down at the desk and called the Medical Records Dept. at the hospital. He enquired about deaths that occurred the night Andy was killed and was told they couldn't release the data unless he was related. He told her he was Philip Warren and was Andrew's only living relative. (Beth's eyebrows rose.) The clerk hesitated and finally put him on hold. Shortly, she picked up and told him he would have to come in person with identification before she could give him the information. *Sounds just like the run-around I got at the paramedic's office,* he thought. He decided to deal with it later.

At nine-fifty, Jim went down to meet up with Manny. The two conversed and Jim told him about the run-around he got from the hospital records clerk.

"Sounds to me like she's had orders not to release any information regarding your friend."

"My thoughts exactly."

Manny continued, "What do you hope to find out at the galleries?"

"I guess I'd like to see what kind of operation they run. From everything I've heard, it promises to be first-class. But I want to see it for myself. If Houseman is there, I will act just like a browsing customer. No names."

"It's my experience that you can learn a lot when you blend into the wall," offered Manny.

"We're on the same page, Manny."

The car dropped Jim at the door and Manny went to look for a parking place. Jim would call him when he wanted picked up.

The entry was lush, with a priceless inlaid mahogany sideboard chest with a pair of porcelain candelabras displayed on top. A handsome card described the candelabras as being Meissen and the chest as a Sheraton. The soup tureen in the middle was also identified. Antiques were *not* Jim's forte. The chest was placed against a glass wall which showed the rear of the candelabras. *Very smart,* thought Jim. *Removes the temptation of an interested customer from handling it.*

He casually moved into the next small entry hall and saw several old English-scrolled signs directing customers to different galleries. One was for Paintings and Sculptures; one for Imported Furniture, and another for Fine Oriental Rugs. Jim chose to investigate the imported furniture gallery.

As he entered the beautiful room, a classy woman approached him, asking in a hushed voice if she could help him. He quietly told her he was looking to furnish an old home he had inherited from a distant relation. He was wanting to use circa late 1800's pieces. He asked her if he could just look around; this was the first gallery he had visited and he wasn't exactly sure what he wanted. She gushed it would be perfectly alright, so Jim slowly sauntered around looking at several pieces. As he traveled, he jotted things down on the pad he carried, pretending interest.

The next gallery he visited was the rooms for Art and Sculptures. He slowly moved up and down the aisles, looking very interested. Surreptitiously, he looked for a sign of an office. There was none to be seen. He did notice several cameras in each gallery realizing they had state-of-the-art security.

Jim's last stop was in the Oriental Rugs section and he saw a multitude of beautiful rugs hanging from racks near the ceiling. He thought, *I should have brought Beth as she would have loved this. Of course, I could always come back; nothing like a beautiful wife on a man's arm to give credence.*

As Jim neared the back of the room, he noticed a door slightly ajar. He nonchalantly began examining the rug closest to the door. He turned it this way and that, even pulling his cell out to take a picture. He stepped closer to the edge of the rug to seemingly get an angled shot. It was a break-room. Sitting at a table were two men drinking coffee. They were ringers for the two men seen entering Andy's apartment by the reception guy. He snapped another picture, seemingly of the rug, but of the two men. He quickly put his phone away and slowly made his way to the front of the building.

The saleslady approached him and asked if he had seen anything he would like for her to price. He told her there were several but he'd have to bring his wife back with him to get her opinion. She gave him her card and asked him to ask for her when he came in; which he promised to do. As he stepped out of the building, he called Manny to come pick him up.

After Jim got into the car, he asked Manny to take him by Stevens' precinct. He wanted to see if the detective intended to tell him he and Beth could move into Andy's apartment today.

The same sergeant was on the front desk. Jim smiled, but got a stone-faced look back. "Can I help you?" barked the man.

"Yes. My name is Jim Redmon and I wondered if I could see Detective Stevens. I don't have an appointment; thought I'd take a chance he was in."

"Sit down over there and I'll call him."

Jim sat in the waiting area again. He was there for about ten or fifteen minutes, which seemed like an hour, and then the sergeant sent him upstairs.

Stevens was waiting for him at the elevator. "What can I do for you, Mr. Redmon?"

He thought, *Do I let him know Philip Warren has told me the police have released Andy's apartment, or do I pretend I'm clueless?* He decided to be upfront with the man and relayed his conversation with Philip.

"If you know the apartment is free for occupation, why come see me?"

"Detective Stevens, I'd like to remind you that you said *you* would call *me* when the police were through with their investigation. After talking with Mr. Warren last night, and since I was in the neighborhood, I decided it would be courteous if I came by to hear it from you. Sorry to waste your time."

Jim turned on his heel and pressed the elevator button.

"Hold on, Redmon. Sorry if I came across rude; come to the break room and let me buy you a cup of coffee."

Stevens wasn't at the top of Jim's list for new friends. But if he played it right, the man could end up being a valuable resource. Jim followed the man down the hall and they found themselves alone in the room. Stevens set a cup of coffee on the table in front of Jim; "cream, sugar?" he asked.

He shook his head. "Black's my preference."

The detective was in uncharted waters. Jim could tell being friendly wasn't his thing. He cleared his throat, "Did you learn anything from your friend's cell phone?"

"Not much," answered Jim. "But I'd like to ask you a question, and I'd appreciate a truthful answer. Did some of your men go through my things in my hotel room? After I got the cell and went out to eat that night, a day later I noticed something had been carefully moved in one of my drawers. I'm not sure when it happened."

By the look on the detective's face, Jim knew this was the first he'd heard about it. So Jim plowed on. "Look, maybe we can work together. It's obvious by the look on your face that you didn't send any men over to my hotel room. There's something fishy going on here and I intend to find out what. . .with or without your help."

Stevens thoughtfully considered the offer. "Let me think about it; I must admit I'm curious about several things concerning this case, but you need to understand that this would be completely against police department rules. I'll call you within 24 hours."

Jim asked the man, "Would you excuse me while I call my friend to come pick me up?"

"Go right ahead."

The phone was answered immediately. "Manny here."

"Hey Manny. I'm ready to go. I'll be in front of the precinct in five minutes."

Stevens spoke up, "That wouldn't be Manny Randolf, would it?"

"Yes. I understand he worked at this precinct once. I've hired him to drive me around while I'm in New York."

"Well I'll be. Small world, isn't it?" Stevens determined to call Manny for his take on Redmon before he entertained sharing any more information with him.

14.
Clean-up

Jim spoke with the Concierge about his plan to leave the hotel during the following week, explaining the situation. The man was most understanding assuring him he could have the suite for as long as necessary. Jim had also contacted the cleaning service to start the following morning. He knew it would take some time to get the apartment back in order before he and Beth could take possession. He had made arrangements for Manny to drive them over in the morning and Beth planned to call Rebecca.

Manny picked up the Redmons for dinner in front of their hotel. Beth looked stunning, as usual, and Jim was pleased for her to meet his new driver. Manny was standing near the passenger side of the car when the couple came out. He wore a nice tan leather jacket and black turtleneck and black dress pants. Beth thought he was handsome.

"Manny, I'd like you to meet Mrs. Redmon."

Manny wasn't prepared for the lovely woman on Jim's arm. "Pleased to meet you, Mrs. Redmon." He glanced at Jim with an approving look.

"Call me Beth, Manny. We aren't very formal and Jim considers you a friend."

Manny thought, *Now here's a first-class southern couple who knows good talent when they see it!* "Okay, you got it, Beth." In a stage voice, Manny announced, "I've got a sweet surprise for you two. You will be dining in one of the best Italian restaurants in the city. Tourists aren't aware of this jewel, so you'll be dining with mainly New Yorkers tonight."

"And you will be joining us, Manny," declared Jim. "You *did* promise to be at my disposal, did you not?" he asked with a smile.

Manny was surprised. "But I don't want to muscle in on you two; you may want a romantic dinner for two. Besides I told a couple of friends I'd have dinner with them."

Jim just shook his head. "It's settled, and I'm sure your friends will understand. Drive on." And they were whisked off to their surprise destination.

The evening was fun and it turned out the owner had made special arrangements for them. It was his pleasure to set another place at their table, for Manny was one of his favorites. Dating back to a time when Manny was a cop, he helped the restaurateur out of a jam. Tonight, he saw to it that they had the best food and service available. Jim had been to a lot of nice restaurants, but this was awesome. The satisfied threesome returned to the hotel with promises from Manny to be ready to pick them up in the morning.

"Not too early, I hope," was Beth's plaintive cry.

"Okay, okay, honey. Come at ten," he instructed his driver. Manny gave him a salute and was off.

Jim needed to call the cleaning service and move their arrival to an hour later. Like Beth, they'd probably be happy, too.

The next morning, Jim lounged around in bed with Beth, ordering room service for breakfast. He told her all about the case and his plans. She asked when he would hear from Detective Stevens, and he replied, "I would presume as soon as he's had a chance to check me out with Manny. That's a given."

In the meantime, that was exactly what Stevens was doing.

"Hey Manny. This is Bob Stevens from the precinct. Hope I didn't call too early."

"Nah, I've been up a couple hours already. What can I do for you Stevens?"

"I understand you're driving Jim Redmon around the city while he's here. Is that right?"

"You got it. I suppose you want me to give you my take on him."

"How'd you guess?"

Manny chuckled. "I think he's a stand-up guy. He's smart, fair, and as far as I can tell, honest. When we discussed my pay, he didn't try to weasel out of paying me a fair wage, which told me a lot about him. Let's see," he considered, "he's a family man, nice wife, two kids in college, and has a successful agency in Tennessee. I also think he's loaded. Seems the guy who was killed is an old army buddy of his and he feels obligated to check into his case. Anything else you need to know?"

"That's as good a reference as I could want. I sure hope he doesn't disappoint you," added Stevens with a touch of sarcasm. He added, "If what you say is *true*, I only wish I could hire him."

"I haven't met many people like him. . .I guess you'd say he's a highly principled man."

While Jim was in the shower, Beth decided to call Rebecca. She looked on Jim's to-do list and found her number.
"Is this Rebecca?" Beth asked.
"Yes. This is Beth, isn't it? I'd know that southern drawl anywhere!"
Beth giggled and told Rebecca the cleaning crew was starting that day and she wondered if Rebecca would be free to come to Andy's apartment. The two women finished with their arrangements just as Jim entered the sitting room.
"I just hung up with Rebecca Langley and she's going to join me at Andy's apartment. I'm sure she'll be a great help in putting things back in order; I'm going to tell the cleaning service to start in the kitchen and bathrooms. While they're busy with that, Rebecca and I can check out the rest of the apartment. When we have a plan, I'll direct the cleaners further."
Too much information, Jim thought. "Sounds like you're getting things arranged just fine without me," he said with a disarming smile.
Beth went on the defensive, saying, "I thought you had more important things to do; I'm just anxious to get the place livable so we can move in."
Jim smoothed his wife's feathers, saying, "I'm delighted you've taken the apartment on. I DO have more important things that cry for my attention. But I want to go through Andy's addresses, files, and check out those lease papers. So I'll probably be at the apartment when Rebecca arrives."
Beth grabbed her coat and purse, saying, "We'd better get a move on; we don't want to keep Manny waiting." Beth had on a pair of jeans, sweatshirt, and sneakers. She carried a change of clothes in a suit bag. She saw Jim's questioning glance and explained, "In case Rebecca and I want to go out for lunch," she said with a sheepish grin. He just smiled, knowing that, too, was a given.
Manny was at the front door. He jumped out and opened the doors for the Redmons. "You don't have to open my door, Manny. I'm perfectly capable, and I can certainly open my wife's door for her."
"Whatever you say, boss."

The car drew up in front of Andy's apartment and the Redmons got out. Jim asked Manny to wait at the curb. He used the key fob for the front door that was provided by Philip when he sent the extra key. As they walked across the lobby, the reception steward's eyes lit up when he recognized Jim.

"Hello, Mr. Redmon. The cleaning service people arrived about ten minutes ago. I let them into the apartment as you instructed."

"Thanks, buddy. We were running a little behind." He approached the reception desk and asked about parking. He gestured toward Manny's car, saying he had hired a driver and, if possible, would like parking privileges. The man told him that every apartment was allotted two spaces. He explained where Mr. Warren's spaces were located and mentioned that Andy's Porsche was still parked there.

"Did the police check out his car?"

"No, I forgot to mention it and didn't think of the car until you just mentioned it."

"Well do me a favor; don't mention it to anyone. I want to check it out before I tell the police."

The Redmons entered Andy's apartment and could hear the cleaning service people in high gear. Beth walked over to one of the men and told him she would like to tell him about where to start. He turned off his vacuum and looked nonplussed, as he'd obviously never heard that before. He couldn't remember ever having people on the site when he and his crew were cleaning up a mess like this. But he stopped immediately and called the other two workers into the room. Beth explained her plan, and they all agreed to tackle the kitchen first, then the bathrooms.

Jim gravitated to Andy's office immediately. He gingerly picked his way through papers, files, and other office paraphernalia over to the desk. Jim admired the old, massive antique and drew the chair up and began methodically going through everything on the surface.

He found the lease right away as it was in the same place where he had photographed it. Jim started reading, finding that Andy had actually signed the lease and paid the first and last month's rent. There was a note, signed by the owner and himself that said "The itemized list of improvements listed below will be done by the landlord before the tenant moves in, date to be decided on by the lessee and landlord. If the landlord does not agree to make the following improvements, the agreement is null and void and all monies will be returned to the tenant, Mr. Andrew Warren." The list followed and both the owner and Andy had signed it. *Good for Andy,* he thought. He intended to go back to the shop and see if those improvements had been made.

He located Andy's insurance coverage for the apartment and called the agent. He explained what had happened, how the cleaning service was there, but assured the man he had pictures of the apartment right after they discovered the break-in. The agent assured him he would come by the next day to assess the situation and any breakage. *Have fun in the kitchen,* Jim thought.

As Jim went through the papers, he tried to file them in reasonable order. He saw all manner of invoices, etc. relating to Andy's business. Then he started looking through the mess on the floor for Andy's rolodex; he wanted to find the addresses of the business associates he had in Europe. When he located it, he pulled out the folder with all the invoices he'd just filed. He saw where Andy had recently made some purchases from a gallery in Paris. In fact, he had highlighted one piece of furniture on the invoice; it was a Louis XV desk. Next to the item, he had written a person's name. Jim thought it was probably the name of a customer.

The doorbell rang, and Jim heard Beth welcoming Rebecca. He went out to greet her. "Hi, Rebecca. Good of you to come over today."

"I'm glad to help, Jim." She looked around, her green eyes wide with surprise. "This place is worse than I thought it'd be! Where do you want me to start, Beth?"

Jim interrupted. "Could you come into the office with me first, Rebecca? I'd like to ask you some questions."

Beth told her she was working in the master bedroom and to join her when she was finished with Jim. Rebecca followed him into the office. She came to a halt just inside the door. "Oh my goodness. This is awful."

"You haven't seen the kitchen yet," he placidly remarked. "But first of all, I'd like to know if you know where Andy kept his spare car key?"

"Yes. He kept it in the small drawer in the table by the front door. I'll go get it for you." She moved to the foyer.

She came back with the key, handing it to Jim. "I guess you know he has a nice Porsche parked in the garage. He seldom used it, but sometimes we would go off someplace special on the weekends." Jim nodded, and pocketed the key. He asked her if Andy had a computer and some questions about Andy's business. She said he had a laptop but didn't know much about the business. There was no sign of a laptop in the apartment.

The doorbell rang again, and shortly Manny appeared at the

office door. "That's one sweet Por. . ." He stopped when he saw Rebecca. Jim could see the look of admiration on his face.

"Hey, Manny, I'd like you to meet Rebecca Langley; Andy's girlfriend. She agreed to help Beth put this place back together, but I've stolen her for a few minutes to ask some questions."

"Glad to meet you, Miss Langley." *Man, this guy surrounds himself with beautiful women!* He looked around the room and asked, "What can I do to help, Jim?"

"I hired you to drive for me, Manny. You don't have to do anything else." But the man wouldn't hear of it and started righting chairs and hanging paintings on the wall."

"Well, if you're sure, you can keep doing what you just did in here! We could use all the help we can get." Manny left the two as they sifted through more business files.

It was a very busy morning and Jim was engrossed in getting the office set up again. His phone rang and it was Detective Stevens. Yes, he decided it would serve them both well to combine their efforts. Could he come by the precinct so they could share information? Jim decided he'd rather have Stevens come to Andy's apartment, *his turf*, and the man agreed. He'd come over around two.

"By the way, detective, could you please bring Warren's computer with you? I forgot all about getting it when we had the cell fiasco." The remark was followed by silence. *He doesn't know anything about a computer,* thought Jim.

Jim was ready for Manny to accompany him down to the garage to look through Andy's car before Stevens got there.

The car was a glossy gray with white leather interior; a beautiful car. They checked the trunk, under the seats, and glove compartment. The laptop was in the trunk; he'd leave it for Stevens to discover. In the glove compartment was a key with the address of Andy's new lease written on a tag attached to it. He pocketed the key and told Manny they might as well leave for lunch while they were in the garage. He alerted him to the fact that Detective Stevens was coming to the apartment around two, so they needed to be back by then.

Meanwhile, Beth and Rebecca had worked in the master bedroom. The service people flipped the mattress for them and Rebecca located a set of sheets. The girls decided to go to lunch and call Manny to pick them up when they were finished. She'd then have him drive them to a store where Beth could buy new pillows and some much-needed groceries. She stepped into the bathroom to change and when she came out, she saw Rebecca curled up on the bed, eyes closed.

"Are you okay, Rebecca?" Beth said with concern.

She sat up immediately and with a sheepish smile remarked, "I don't know what's gotten into me. I guess it's because I haven't worked like this in ever so long." She stood, and straightened her blouse.

"We don't have to go to lunch, and you most assuredly don't have to come back here today." Beth looked at the young woman and realized she was quite flushed. "Are you sure you're okay?"

"Sure. Let's go to lunch. I'll probably bounce back with some food in my stomach. I didn't eat breakfast."

The guy at the front desk called them a cab and they were off to the restaurant of Rebecca's choice.

Stevens arrived soon after the men were back at the apartment. He was pleased to see Manny and Jim were on friendly terms.

The three went down to the garage, and Stevens went through the car thoroughly. Jim and Manny were attentive, but knew Stevens would find the computer eventually. When he did, he looked Jim's way and said, "I wondered about a computer when you mentioned it to me. I knew it wasn't logged in, but look at the mess we had with the cell phone. Let's take the computer back upstairs and try to find out what's on it." Jim sensed a thaw in Stevens.

They returned to the apartment and spent the better part of an hour sifting through Andy's computer. It yielded nothing of value for their case. A dead end.

15.
New Developments

It was a beautiful day for New York in February. The temperature was in the high forties and sunny. The ladies were seated, having just finished their lunch; Rebecca left hurriedly for the Ladies Room. When she returned, Beth looked at the stricken, pale look on Rebecca's face.

Beth waited a moment, while the young woman was seated. She looked at her closely, and asked, "Are you pregnant, Rebecca?"

Rebecca burst into tears. She just nodded her head.

Beth called for the check, had the restaurant call them a cab, and hustled Rebecca out the door as quickly as she could. She told the cabbie to take her to Andy's building but Rebecca blubbered, "No. I want to go home."

After the two women were seated in Rebecca's gorgeous condo, she spoke quietly. "I knew I was pregnant over a month ago, Beth. I think it happened the middle part of November." She glanced at her hands, "The evening Andy was hit by that car, I had a speech prepared to give him that very night. I was going to tell him I wanted out of the relationship!" She wiped a tear. "Little did I know that I had no choice in the matter.

"I had already made up my mind that this baby would be kept a secret from Andy for I didn't want him to think I set out to trap him into marrying me. You see, it was my *plan* to get pregnant because I knew it was now or never. I'm getting up there; late thirties. I wanted a child, Andy's baby, because I loved him so completely and I thought he was a kind, honest man. I willfully stopped taking my birth control pills about four months ago knowing full well the hard path I was headed. It was a heart-wrenching decision to break up with him, and I cried all the time."

"Did you ever consider going to this extreme with your husband?"

"I thought about it, but I knew things weren't right with us. I can remember looking at him with a clinical eye one day and realized he didn't have the traits I would like any child of mine to have. It wasn't long after, he served me with divorce papers. I was shocked, because I didn't expect it, and hurt because he said he didn't love me anymore. I was so thankful I didn't try to get pregnant."

"Oh Rebecca. I'm so sorry." Beth reached over and clasped her hand which brought on a new rush of tears. "Have you told anyone?" she asked.

Rebecca shook her head. "You're the first one I've told." My mother has been dead for a long time; my dad lives in Oregon. He's moved on with his life, remarried, has two kids in high school, and I only hear from him at Christmas and on my birthday. I've seen him once in the last seven years. We have no relationship."

Beth hurt for her new friend. "Have you been to a doctor yet?"

"Yes. I went to my GYN and he confirmed I was pregnant. He gave me the name of a good obstetrician but I haven't felt like calling; in fact, I haven't felt like doing anything. All I seem to do is sleep!"

"Sounds to me like you need to call that doctor today. You've suffered a terrible shock, on top of the pregnancy, and I sense from what you tell me you could be suffering from depression. You *need* to be under a doctor's care, Rebecca; for your sake *and* the baby." She patted the woman's hand. "Let me help you while I'm here. I can call the doctor's office and set up an appointment for you. And I'll go with you."

"Would you do that for a perfect stranger?"

"Of course I would. Tell me the doctor's name and where the phone book is kept."

After the appointment was made, Beth disappeared into the kitchen. When she returned with a pot of tea, she spoke quietly, with concern. "You know Rebecca, there are pregnant women whose husbands are in the military on active duty and some of those men never return. Essentially, those gals are in the same situation you're in. It's terrible, it's sad, and it stinks, but it's a fact of life. Now let's make some pleasant plans for this little one."

Beth called Manny to pick her up at Rebecca's apartment. He was surprised to see the opulent building where Rebecca lived; *the high rent district*, he called it. As he waited on the circular drive, the doorman opened Beth's door and Manny whisked her away to a grocery store.

When they returned with the groceries, they took the elevator from the parking garage. The two of them struggled toward the door, laden with grocery bags. When she approached the door, Jim was waiting, having been alerted by Manny.

"Stevens just left," he remarked, as he headed to the kitchen with Beth's bags. "He was here about an hour and I think the time was productive for both of us." He looked over his shoulder at Manny, "I'm taking your word that he's a straight-shooter."

"And you won't be sorry. Of course, I would imagine he'd be more agreeable in sharing about the case after he's had a chance to size you up."

"Yeah, I got that impression. I can't fault him as I feel the same way. Right now we're taking it slow; like two animals circling one another trying to figure out what's what."

Beth stayed in the kitchen and put things away. She was thankful the kitchen was so clean, just waiting for someone to fill it up.

Jim motioned Manny to come into Andy's office. "I'd like to run some things by you that Stevens told me and get your take on it." The two sat down in the sitting area near the window. There was still plenty to do in this room; junk on the floor, a couple lamp shades all bent out of shape, and a good vacuuming was needed after removing a spilled planter. Jim had just about filed all the papers in their rightful place, and the desk was ready for polishing. The service was coming in the morning to finish up.

"The more open I was with Stevens, the more he seemed to relax, sharing more info with me. I believe we'll be able to work together."

"Did he give you anything helpful?"

"He's uneasy about one of the cops on the graveyard shift of the property desk, but he hasn't finished his investigation yet. I, in turn, told him about the Houseman Galleries. He liked the idea of keeping my connection with the Warren family a secret. And he also encouraged me to go back with Beth and maybe get a good look at Houseman."

"Did you tell him about the two goons you saw over there?"

"I did. That really seemed to interest him. He's going to see if he can look at a copy of the security tapes from the street directly in front of the gallery and one of the alley in back."

Manny didn't want to seem like he was barging in where he wasn't needed, but he asked the question anyway. "Do you think he might have an idea who 'Foster' is? I think that would be a good place to start."

"I didn't mention the name because I'm waiting to hear back from Dave. With his connections, he may be able to help me. I have a gut feeling that Foster is working with a government agency. I have perfect faith in Andy's integrity and I know he wouldn't do anything illegal. In the meantime, Stevens asked if he thought we could tail one of the goons from the galleries." With a grin, he went on. "I told him I thought we could arrange that."

Beth came in with coffee on a tray. "I thought you two could use a cup."

After enjoying their coffee, Manny asked if he'd be needed for the evening. Both Jim and Beth agreed they'd enjoy a relaxed evening in their room and decided to go back to the hotel and order room service. Tomorrow would be a busy day moving to the apartment and settling in.

16.
Tales

Over dinner, Beth told Jim all about her afternoon with Rebecca. He was shocked and concerned. "When is she to see the doctor?" he asked.

"Next Monday. I explained to the nurse about Rebecca's age, her signs of depression, and about the baby's father dying. She was very kind and worked Rebecca in on Monday morning. I'll be going with her."

"Good, I think you should. Does she have family in New York?" When Beth told him the situation with Rebecca's family, he was even more concerned. "Tough break!"

The couple talked with their kids, catching up with all that was going on in their lives. Emily was looking forward to a ski trip for winter break, and Trey talked with his dad about his rotation; that he was seriously considering changing directions rather than research. "Have you talked with your grandfather about it?" Jim inquired.

"Yes. He told me I was the only one who could choose but he'd help with any questions I may have." Beth's father, a physician, had always been one of Trey's idols. When the couple hung up, they both remarked how thankful they were for a loving family; especially knowing the heartache Rebecca was experiencing.

The following morning, after bringing their luggage in, the Redmons sat down in Andy's plush living room and planned their day. As they chatted, Andy's phone rang. It surprised Jim, and he rushed into the office to answer it.

"Hello."

"I'm calling from Tiffany's to tell you your order is ready, Mr. Warren. When can you come in to pick it up?"

Jim was surprised. "This is Jim Redmon; I'm sure you haven't heard the sad news yet, but Mr. Warren was killed in an auto accident recently. I'm a close friend of his."

The man was incredulous. "Oh, I'm so sorry! Mr. Warren came

in about three weeks ago and placed an order with us for a ring. He had some specific changes as to the size of the diamond, and we just got it back. I guess this means he won't need it now." He paused, "Is that the right assumption?"

"I'm sorry to say you are right. Who am I speaking to?" asked Jim.

The man gave his name and added that Mr. Warren had paid a significant deposit on the ring. "To whom should I return the deposit?"

Jim told him he would advise him after he had a chance to talk with Mr. Warren's uncle, his only surviving relative. The conversation ended and Jim walked into the bedroom where Beth was hanging up clothes. "You won't believe who was on the phone!" He told her the gist of the conversation, adding, "Please don't say anything to Rebecca yet. We need to find the right time."

Shortly after lunch, Jim got a call from Dave Weinbtroub. "You got anything for me, Dave?"

"The FBI was working with Andy and from what I understand, I think Andy became suspicious of that gallery he used. The guy who was advising him is an agent by the name of Bruce Foster. Everything is very hush-hush, so don't mention any of this to anyone. I know how you feel about keeping secrets from Beth, but this is one time I would ask you to keep the information to yourself. What she doesn't know won't hurt her, it's that serious."

"Copy that. Is Foster here in New York?"

"Yes, but I very much doubt they know what he's working on. In fact, I would say there aren't many people privy to what's going on. Jim, this is *big*. I had to practically sign in blood that I wouldn't carry this information further." He laughed with derision, "And here I am telling you!"

"I appreciate it, Dave. I need answers to many questions regarding this case. But knowing that Andy was in cahoots with an FBI agent does give me a clue as to what could be going on."

Per earlier arrangements, Manny drove Jim to get his gun permit. After they left the building, Jim slipped his gun and holster on. The two picked up lunch and drove by the gallery. The Mercedes was nowhere to be seen, however, a dark van was parked behind the building.

"I sure would like to check out the inside of that vehicle," Jim muttered.

"Have you and Beth decided when you're going to visit the gallery?"

"No, but I'd like to be sure Houseman is there because he's the only reason I want to visit the gallery again."

"Maybe I could call to make an appointment with Houseman?" suggested Manny.

"That's a great idea. Then Beth and I could arrive right after you did."

Jim told Manny to set it up. He knew Beth was going somewhere with Rebecca for the day, so he suggested Manny try to get an appointment for the following day. The two came up with the idea of Manny pretending to be an importer that wanted to make arrangements with the galleries to rent space. He knew Houseman wouldn't be interested, but it served the purpose of making sure the man was on the premises.

Jim called Stevens to see if he'd had any luck with the security tapes. He was busy and couldn't talk but promised to call that afternoon.

Jim and Manny stopped at a small bar for some beers. The two started brain-storming about what was next. "I need to talk to Dave again and find out what he suggests we do about Foster. I *need* to talk to that guy," Jim stated.

"Speaking of making calls," interjected Manny, "I think I'll call the galleries now and see about getting that appointment with Houseman." Manny was on a roll and opened his cell and found the number, calling immediately.

"Yes, I'd like to speak with Mr. Houseman, please."

The receptionist told him Mr. Houseman wasn't in and would he like to leave his name and number.

"My name is Manfred Rudolf and I'm calling to make an appointment with Mr. Houseman as soon as possible. Would you know if he has any time to see me tomorrow?"

Jim was amazed at how deftly the information rolled off Manny's tongue. *Manfred Rudolf? Give me a break,* he thought. It dawned on him, *He's done this before!*

"Why yes, he doesn't have anything scheduled between two and four tomorrow afternoon," said the young woman. "Shall I put you down for 2:30, Mr. Rudolf?"

"Yes. I'll be there."

The two men decided to make another run by the gallery. They hit the bull's eye, for the Mercedes was there. As they drove by, a man exited the building and approached the car. Manny could see in his rearview mirror that he fit the description of one of the men seen entering Andy's apartment the day the apartment was robbed.

"I hate to circle the block in case our car grabs the guy's attention."

Jim agreed with him. They kept moving with traffic but pulled into a *Deliveries Only* space in front of a building down the block.

"We need to follow him if he leaves," instructed Jim.

"Agreed."

It didn't take long to see that the man was pulling out. He had his cell to his ear, obviously interested in his conversation and the traffic. It was okay with Jim; it would allow them to follow with less chance of being spotted.

The drive was uneventful with Manny changing lanes occasionally. The Mercedes glided along the streets of Manhattan, finally changing directions to the warehouse district. Manny hung back more, as there was very little traffic. The car finally came to a fenced warehouse site and stopped in front of the gate. He pushed an automatic opener and slowly entered the property. Jim thought, *I wonder if this is where Houseman keeps his incoming merchandise?*

The two kept driving at a normal speed, noticing that the guy driving the Mercedes seemed to be oblivious to their presence.

Manny took a hard right at the next corner. Jim was surprised.

"I think we have company and I intend to find out for sure."

"Go for it," Jim responded.

They made a few more turns, and the sedan hung back but turned after them.

"I think you're right, Manny. There's only one guy in the car and he's definitely tailing us. I have an idea, drive me to Stevens' precinct and as soon as we get close, drop me off "

When the car stopped, Jim jumped out and ran up the steps before the guy in the sedan could see him. Manny made like he was looking for a parking spot, but quickly circled the block and caught up with the sedan. The guy didn't realize their roles had changed. Manny called Jim and read off the license plate number.

After Jim reached the front desk, he asked if he could see Detective Stevens, and gave his name. Stevens quickly came down to get him.

The detective shook hands, saying, "I'm surprised to see you," as he led the way to the elevator.

Jim told him he'd like to share some information with him in private. With that, the two disappeared into a conference room where Jim relayed what had just happened and how they had followed the Mercedes to the industrial district. He supplied the address, and Stevens wrote it down. "This is the license number Manny just gave me. Can you check it out?"

"Sure, come back with me to my desk."

It took a while, but Stevens finally had something. "It's a government issue but i'm not sure what agency. At any rate, someone is keeping a tight reign on what goes on at the gallery. Do you and your wife have plans for going over there?"

"As a matter of fact, we're going tomorrow afternoon."

The detective looked hard at Jim. "I guess you don't need me to warn you to be careful."

Jim nodded. The two parted and Jim had Manny pick him up on the corner.

Jim decided to see if he could get some more information from the Medical Records Dept at the hospital. They swung by Andy's apartment so Jim could grab some things. Manny noticed the transformation as Jim got back into the car. He carried Andy's briefcase, wore a nice coat and tie and Manny drove him to the hospital. He presented himself at the appropriate desk and asked politely to speak to someone in charge of death records.

"I can help you," spoke an elderly lady.

Jim nodded with a smile. "I'm the attorney for a man who was brought to this hospital on the night of February 4th. I need a copy of his death certificate to proceed in finalizing his estate. For some reason, my secretary called several times but the hospital couldn't supply it. I thought the best thing was to come down here in person to handle it."

"Of course," said the woman. "What is the deceased's name?"

After Jim gave all the information, the clerk left the counter and disappeared into the room behind. He waited for at least ten minutes before she returned.

"I'm sorry, but I have no record of an Andrew Warren dying in this facility on the date you gave me. Could he have been moved to another hospital?"

"No. The family was told he died en route to this hospital. I am very concerned about this situation and would like to speak to your supervisor."

The woman quickly disappeared and came back with a tall man in tow. He asked, "Can I help you?"

Jim explained once again and the man tried to pacify him. He could not explain it, but there was no record of Andy dying in that hospital, or any medical doctor signing a death certificate after Andrew Warren was supposedly brought in. He suggested Jim go to the ambulance company for more information.

Jim thanked the gentleman and left. He relayed the whole scenario to Manny. As they rehashed what had happened that day, they both agreed they needed to work something out so they could change cars occasionally. Manny said he had an old truck and his son's Mustang parked in his garage. He figured his son wouldn't mind him using his car now and then. He decided to call it a cheap storage fee.

Jim added, "Andy's Porsche is in the garage at the apartment. I think Beth and I will use it to go the gallery tomorrow."

When they arrived back at Andy's, Jim determined to ask Rebecca if he could park Andy's car in her garage. That would free up two spaces for Manny's cars. As he unlocked the door, he could see Beth and Rebecca in the living room going through packages piled high on the coffee table.

"Well hi you two. By the looks of all those bags, I see you've had a productive day." He gestured toward the table and smiled when he saw the beaming look on Rebecca's face.

"We've shopped 'til we dropped," answered Beth. "We had a ball going through baby departments at the best stores in Manhattan. And to put the icing on the cake, in a couple of days they're going to deliver a crib and stroller to Rebecca."

"I'm glad you found so much." He turned to Rebecca and said, "It makes it all more real, doesn't it?

She nodded shyly.

"Rebecca, would it be alright for me to park Andy's car in your parking garage?"

She looked surprised. "I'm sure it'll be alright. Why?"

"I'm going to need a place for Manny to park two other vehicles. We need them for my business."

Sensing that was all he was going to say, Rebecca asked, "When should I advise my building manager?"

"As soon as you get home would be great."

"You've got it," she said, turning back to open yet another package.

Jim strolled into the kitchen and had some milk and cookies. He smiled. *His wife thought of everything, even buying his favorite chocolate chips and 2% milk.* As he was taking his glass to the sink, his phone rang.

"Redmon here."

"Jim, it's Dave. I'm returning to New York tomorrow and wondered if we could have dinner?"

"Sure, buddy. I was going to call you. What time?" They set a time and place.

17.
The Gallery

Friday morning, the cleaning service came and finished up. Shortly after they left, the insurance agent called apologizing for not showing up on Wednesday. He made a vague excuse and asked if it would be alright if he came now. Jim told him to come ahead, then alerted the guy at the reception desk. Things were perking right along, and it wasn't even ten o'clock.

After the agent left, Beth rustled up a tasty lunch in Andy's clean kitchen. They chatted and Beth decided since Jim was having dinner with Dave, she'd invite Rebecca to join her for dinner. Would it be okay to enlist Manny for the evening? Jim surprised her and said no. He heard Manny making plans with friends for the evening and he wanted him to feel free to go.

"That's okay," she said, "we can easily take a cab."

Manny called and made arrangements to meet Jim back at Andy's after their trips to the gallery.

"Would you mind meeting us at Rebecca's? It'll save us some time if I can park the Porsche there."

"Sounds like a plan," agreed Manny.

Jim did paperwork and Beth read a book until it was time for her to freshen up to go to the gallery. Her husband had given her the heads up about their story. She was ready; after all this was exciting and she felt like a real live spy.

The sleek Porsche glided into the parking lot. Manny had already arrived, for Jim saw the Mustang parked a few spots away. The couple entered the gallery and Manny was standing at the desk flirting with the receptionist; an attractive girl around thirty. She was enjoying his attention, but quickly became businesslike when the Redmons walked in. Manny sat down in the waiting area.

Jim handed the receptionist the saleswoman's card and asked if she was in. "Do you have an appointment?" When he told her no, she said, "I'll call her and see if she's with a customer." In a moment, she told Jim the saleslady would be right up. She looked coyly at Manny and said, "Mr. Houseman is on his way, Mr. Rudolf." Jim prayed he would come before their saleslady appeared.

Within minutes, a tall, middle aged man entered the lobby. He had dark hair and a beard. He approached Manny with an outstretched hand; the picture of *friendly*. He introduced himself as Fred Houseman and would Manny kindly follow him to his office. As Manny followed Houseman, Jim was proud of his attention to detail; he had on a dark business suit with a white shirt and tie; a tan overcoat over his arm. He looked affluent. After the two men left, the saleslady came in to collect her customers.

Soon the Redmons were being escorted around the gallery with a knowledgeable saleswoman. Jim looked at his notes from the time before, and asked her to show Mrs. Redmon those items. They began their trek through the gallery. Beth uttered her oohs and aahs appropriately, and then they entered the rug section. Jim was most anxious to see if the two men were in the break room, but the door was closed. He pulled the rug forward that he had looked at the last time. Just as he was telling Beth that this was the one that caught his eye, the door to the break room opened. Jim hastily turned his back to the person leaving the room. Beth started asking pertinent questions about the rug's origin, etc. Jim could have kissed her.

The man leaving matched the description of one of the men seen leaving Andy's apartment the day of the break-in. The saleslady seemed oblivious to the man as he exited the room. She went on with her spiel with no interruption.

Jim and Beth stayed with the woman until they had all the information they could possibly need. Beth remarked, "The rug is beautiful, but I'm not about to choose one until I know the colors I want to use. I'll definitely keep this one in mind; it's perfect!" The woman nodded knowingly. Beth asked her, with her most charming smile, "Would you mind if we just browsed awhile?"

"Of course. Feel free to roam throughout our galleries. If you find something of interest, just call me." She pointed to the entryway. "There's a buzzer on the doorpost at each entrance of all the galleries. You reach the receptionist by pressing it once. If you press it twice, you will reach me. I'll be glad to price anything for you." With that, she courteously withdrew hoping this visit would materialize into a hefty commission.

"Pretty classy place," whispered Beth.

Jim replied in a whisper of his own. "Now we get to pretend we're really interested in checking things out. I pinpointed the security cameras the last time I was here and it might be suspicious if we left right away."

The couple spent about thirty more minutes looking around, with Jim making more notations on his pad they never intended to use. They smiled and thanked the receptionist as they left.

After parking the Porsche, Jim and Beth rode to the first floor of Rebecca's building. From the lobby, they could see Manny waiting outside in the drive.

Jim immediately started asking Manny. "Tell me, off the top of your head, what do you think of Houseman?"

"He's very professional and, as you saw, is a meticulous dresser. I took note of the pictures on his credenza. There was a woman I presumed to be his wife, and two kids, a boy and girl. His wife was a beauty with large eyes, and his son must be around 12 or 13; his daughter is probably seven or eight. They look middle eastern to me."

"Was it a portrait?" Jim asked.

"No. I think it was taken in a yard with a pool off to the side. I'm sure it was probably at someone's house."

"How did the conversation start?" Jim inquired.

"He wanted to know what made me think he was renting space. And he also asked me who had told me about his gallery." Manny glanced Jim's way. "I told him I had spoken to a couple antique dealers I knew and asked for their recommendation. Both had wholeheartedly given me the name of the Houseman Galleries but wasn't sure if they allowed other dealers to rent space.

"He asked me some more questions about my product line, and I'm glad I did some research last night. It gave me credibility. Anyway, he explained he wasn't interested in renting out space but would keep my name if he ever changed his mind." Jim commented, "It looks like that was a waste. But I DID get a look at him and I agree with you, he looks like he could be a middle easterner."

18.
Try, Try Again

After returning to the apartment, Beth went right to the bedroom to take a nap. *This cloak and dagger stuff is tiring,* she thought.

Jim called Stevens to report on their trip to the gallery. "One thing I can tell you, he is an affluent businessman who looks good in his designer suit. He looks like he could be middle eastern, and Manny had a chance to sit down and talk with him in his office. He said Houseman appears to have a wife and two kids, according to pictures on his credenza.

"Beth and I went on a shopping tour with a saleslady and while we were looking at oriental rugs, I got a chance to see one of the guys seen leaving Andy's apartment; at least he fits the description. He isn't the bald guy in the twosome; I guess this guy had the suit on when seen leaving Andy's."

Stevens seemed pleased that Jim had thought to call him as soon as he arrived home. He informed Jim he had a chance to meet Mercer who works the graveyard shift on the Property Desk.

"He told me nothing of value. He said it was quiet the night Warren's personal effects were brought in and he listed them as he was supposed to do. When he finished, he sealed them in an envelope with his name on it. He has no idea why the cell wasn't included; as a matter of fact, he couldn't recall whether there was a cell or not. I got the definite impression he knows more but isn't telling. I've got some ideas and will let you know when I have something."

Jim and Manny discussed several ideas to get more information from the ambulance company. They decided Manny would play the role of a police officer. He had a replica of his old police badge in the glove compartment and Jim decided not to question. He planned to walk brazenly into the reception area with a believable story to get information.

"I'd like to speak to the manager. I'm Detective Manny Randolf with the NYPD," he said as he flashed his ID.

"Just a moment," said a young man who sat behind the desk.

Shortly a heavy-set woman appeared and shot an arm out to shake hands. "I'm the manager and who might you be?' she said with good humor.

"I'm Manny Randolf with the NYPD and I need some information about a hit-and-run call your company responded to on the night of February 4th." He could see the consternation that crossed her face.

"I'm not at liberty to share any information about that call, Detective Randolf. We were instructed by the FBI to deny any information to anyone who inquired about the case. I'm sorry."

"Damn!" Manny played the role of the angry police officer well as he continued, "I wish they'd get their facts straight before sending us to get information that they know will be denied to us! Someone is going to get a piece of my mind when I get back to headquarters." He stormed out of the office.

Jim and Manny considered the information that Manny got. "So it IS the FBI who's running this show," commented Jim. "This is all starting to make more sense.

The two bantered the information about for a short time and then Jim gave Manny the weekend off. He asked him to come by on Monday morning. "And you don't have to come before nine," Jim declared, which suited Manny just fine.

Saturday and Sunday were spent in a relaxing mode for both Jim and Beth. On Saturday, they did some sightseeing, eating out, and a little shopping. . .which wasn't one of Jim's favorite things but he *was* curious about the biggest Macy's in the world. Sunday afternoon, Jim called Philip Warren to report on what was happening. He knew the elderly man was probably chomping at the bit for information.

"Hello, Philip? This Jim Redmon. I wanted to give you an update about Andy's case. . ."

Monday morning found Beth cleaning up after a bounteous breakfast. She had to get dressed and ready to go with Rebecca to the doctor's office. She knew they were in for a long wait; doctor's offices didn't fit people in easily with an already busy schedule.

Manny arrived promptly and Jim told him they were going to run by and see Stevens as soon as the cop called them. The two went into Andy's office and talked about the new information they had over a cup of coffee..

"I've been doing some wishful thinking," said Manny. "It would be nice if we knew someone in the local FBI office we could pump for information."

Jim smiled to himself, thinking of his friend Dave, who had already found out about Bruce Foster. He couldn't share the information with Manny, even though he trusted him. If Dave asked him specifically not to even share with Beth, he knew anyone else was out of the question.

The phone rang and the two sleuths left for Steven's precinct.

Jim decided to take Manny up to Stevens' office with him. He had become an integral part of Jim's investigation. The two were welcomed by Stevens and he brought them up to speed.

"Ralph Mercer is on the property desk for the graveyard shift. He's the main one I've been checking on. He had a cop named George Hadi pull some strings for him to get him on the property desk." Stevens directed his attention to Manny. "As you know, it isn't easy to get on that desk. I looked into Hadi's record and found he had some favors owed him because of an important bust he helped bring about. I asked his superior about him and he told me he was a polite, well-liked man who seemed to want to succeed at his job. He was presently studying for his detective's badge. He told me he had never had any complaints about him and wanted to know why I was asking. I hedged that question without ever really answering him." He looked at both men.

"I asked him if he knew anything about Hadi's personal life and he said he knew he was a practicing Muslim but never foisted his faith on others. He had a wife and two boys in high school and his wife was from Jordan."

Jim's mind was racing. *Here's a possible connection to the Houseman Galleries and the middle easterner, Fred Houseman.* "Would you happen to know where he lives?"

"In a heavily Muslim populated area of Brooklyn. Other than that, I know nothing more about him."

Jim was very pleased to get the information. He had a gut feeling all of this was connected to Andy in some way. How, he wasn't sure but he intended to find out.

19.
Surprise, Surprise

As requested, Beth and Rebecca arrived at the office fifteen minutes early to fill out forms. After about a 45 minute wait, Rebecca was sent to get her lab work done. After that, she was sent to an examining room where Dr. Randall did an exam. While they were in the examining room, the lab results came back and the pregnancy was confirmed. She was asked to dress and wait for the doctor in her office.

"Could my friend join me?" she asked the nurse. "She was sitting with me in the waiting room."

The nurse was the one Beth had talked to when she made Rebecca's appointment and knew the patient was probably nervous and could use the moral support. She quickly returned to the waiting room and brought Beth back with her. The two waited for another ten minutes before the doctor came in. Beth guessed she was probably in her early fifties with a maternal appearance.

After the introductions, Dr. Randall asked Rebecca to tell her about her medical history. She opened up and probably revealed more than the doctor wanted to know. The woman was a very good listener and responded to Rebecca kindly. Beth considered this doctor an answer to prayer for Rebecca. She felt she was in good hands.

Dr. Randall explained they needed an ultrasound performed because of Rebecca's age. This needed to be completed before she could tell Rebecca how many weeks she was into her pregnancy. She also wanted to check her fluid levels and wondered if Rebecca was free to have them done now.

After a nod from Beth, Rebecca shyly responded, "I'm free today if you want to get started."

The day was long and the two women were in the office much longer than they planned. But it was worth it for by the time they left, Rebecca knew she was in her thirteenth week, she had an appointment to see someone about her depression, and was put on a good-eating and vitamin regimen. She was to see the doctor again in three weeks.

On their way out, the two went directly to a lunch counter in the building. Beth knew Rebecca needed to eat. The mom-to-be was bubbly and thrilled with the outcome of her doctor's visit. Beth felt the same way for her, and the two made plans to get together within the week. . .to shop for maternity clothes, of course.

When Jim returned that afternoon, he called out for Beth and realized she hadn't returned yet. He went into the kitchen for his cookies and milk break (which he realized had to stop if he wanted to wear the clothes in his closet). His cell phone rang.

"Hello."

A man's voice asked, "Is this Jim Redmon?"

"This is Redmon."

"My name is Agent Bruce Foster with the FBI."

Jim sat down hard on one of the counter stools. This was the last person in the world he expected to hear from.

The agent continued, "I'd like to meet with you as soon as possible. I think you know what this is about."

"Yes, yes of course. When and where?" Jim uttered.

"I know you're staying in Andy's apartment and wondered if it would be okay for us to meet there this evening?"

"It would be fine with me but I'm sure you realize my wife is here with me."

"And I'm sure you realize we could talk privately in Andy's office."

Jim had learned a lot about Bruce Foster just from this phone call. One, he knew he was staying at Andy's apartment. Two, he referred to his friend as "Andy", so there was some familiarity between the two. Three, he'd been in Andy's apartment because he knew the privacy Andy's office offered.

"Tonight would be fine," Jim replied. "And we can meet here."

The first thing Jim needed to do was call Dave and reschedule. Dave was receptive to going out for lunch the next day.

This meeting with Foster ought to be interesting, speculated Jim. The time had been set for eight o'clock. Beth's plans to have dinner with Rebecca had fallen through. The young woman said she was just too tired. He knew Beth wouldn't mind watching television or reading her book and she had decided to retire to the bedroom, looking forward to watching a couple of her favorite TV shows. As Jim checked on her, he saw she was in her robe propped up on many pillows in the massive king bed. She looked so comfortable, he wished he could join her.

When the bell from downstairs rang, Jim was waiting at the door when the man stepped off the elevator. Jim sized him up, seeing a man he guessed was in his early forties, with a mop of brown hair. He was dressed casually.

Jim reached out to shake hands and greeted his guest. "I can honestly say I'm glad to meet you," he said with a smile. "I'm Jim Redmon."

"Glad to meet you; Bruce Foster."

They entered the apartment and Jim offered drinks, but Foster declined. They walked into Andy's office and Jim closed the door. He gestured toward the two chairs near the window. "Have a seat."

The two were checking one another out.

Jim said, "Why don't you start, since you called this meeting."

The man was nervous. "I'd like to answer some of the questions I'm sure you have, so why don't we begin there."

Jim jumped right in. "Who or what did we bury on February 8th?"

Foster smiled, "You get right to the point, don't you?"

"Seemed the question to ask because that's where it all began for me."

"Let me give you some of the facts of what happened leading up to the night in question. Andy was kidnapped by a faction that he suspected of doing some dangerous and illegal stuff. I'm sure he didn't think they suspected him of figuring it all out and was probably shocked when they picked him up. He had called the FBI when he discovered a cache of large diamonds in one of his imported pieces about a month ago. When he mentioned the Houseman Galleries to us, the bosses sat up and took notice. They assigned me to covertly work with Andy as we've had the galleries under surveillance for a long time now."

Jim's mind was in overdrive and he didn't know what questions he wanted to ask next. "Of course, I had no idea about all of this and was suspicious of the galleries. But my first and foremost concern is to find out about Andy. Is he alive?"

"He sustained a serious beating and they thought he was dead when he was pushed out of a vehicle. We scooped him up when one of our agents told us about how his body had been thrown out of a car, called 9-1-1, and how he'd been picked up by an emergency medical unit. We found out they were taking him to

Belleview. Our agents took it from there and everyone assumed Andy was dead." He paused. "You're the only one who has questioned that."

Foster continued, "My boss was so aggravated with you! You seemed to be nosing around everywhere we didn't want you to be. After you hired that ex-cop to drive you around, things *really* started to unravel quickly. We figured we needed to read you in, so here I am giving you the whole story."

"I'm not completely satisfied. I assume Andy is alive, but where is he and what kind of shape is he in?"

"Would you like to take a ride with me this evening, Mr. Redmon?"

"Call me Jim, and yes I'd like to take a ride but I need to tell my wife I'm leaving. Do you know approximately how long we'll be?"

"We should be back around midnight."

Jim explained to Beth and the two men left.

20.
Recovery

Bruce drove directly into Queens. He stopped outside a modest home with no lights to be seen. The two approached the porch and Bruce knocked on the door.

"That you, Foster?"

"Yeah. I've got Redmon with me."

The door swung open and a man stood there with his hand on his holster. He nodded at the two visitors.

Foster spoke, "How's he doing tonight?"

"I believe he turned the corner. Was awake for about ten minutes earlier, and then has been snoozing ever since."

Bruce Foster turned around to look at Jim and said, "This is Vince; Vince this is Jim Redmon; a good friend of Andy's." He paused, "He'll be working with me."

The two men shook hands.

Foster told Jim to follow him upstairs and they approached a door at the end of the hall. It was a strange house, as far as Jim was concerned. It looked like the movie set of a home from the 70's. Beyond the door, at the end of the hall, was a desk with a young woman seated.

"Hi, Mandy. How's our patient doing tonight?"

"Resting peacefully. Dr. Keel came by and took some of the bandages off his head earlier today and said he was healing quickly. I think you'll be pleasantly surprised when you see him."

"Can I talk to him?"

"Well, he's sleeping right now but due for meds shortly. If you don't mind waiting, that would be better. I want him to sleep as much as possible."

"Fine. Got any fresh decaf in the kitchen?"

"Yes. Help yourself. I'll come get ya'll after I've given him his shot."

The two men made themselves at home in the kitchen area and sat down to wait. Jim asked, "Is the nurse on your payroll?"

"Yes. She's new and just arrived from Tennessee a couple months ago. She's a knowledgeable top-notch nurse. After she got out of nursing school, she worked for a short time in a prison in Tennessee. She worked there only six months and hated it. She felt that was enough time to satisfy her desire to pay her dues. We were looking for a good nurse with clearance and when her resume was red-flagged, we talked with her. The elevated salary we pay helped swing the decision in our favor. Her husband is just out of medical school and is doing his rotations at Bellevue. Hence the move to NYC."

Foster looked at Jim. "Tennessee! That's where you're from, isn't it?"

Jim nodded. He was amazed Bruce Foster knew where he was from, and who knew what else. It made him a bit uneasy and he didn't like being in that position.

It wasn't long before Mandy appeared and told them they could go up and see Andy. They deposited their cups in the sink and followed her up the stairs.

Jim stepped into the dimmed room. He saw Andy's form on the hospital bed with a drip attached to his arm. He approached the bed and laid his hand on Andy's. His touch provoked a response from Andy; he opened his eyes slightly. After only a moment, Andy's eyes grew wide and he tried to speak.

"You don't have to say anything, buddy. I'm here and you're on the mend." He motioned Bruce to come closer, "Foster and I are going to work together to try to find out who's behind all this. You just get stronger and we'll talk later."

With that, Jim turned to leave the room. He heard a soft voice behind him, "What about Rebecca?" the patient croaked, his voice box not yet working.

Jim turned. "She's as good as can be expected. Beth and I have seen her often and are helping her get through this." He paused and cautiously said, "She thinks you're dead, Andy." With that, Andy's eyes welled and once again he closed his eyes.

They walked downstairs and said their goodbyes. Then, Bruce promised Vince he'd be back in a couple of days but said he'd be calling every afternoon for a report on Andy's progress.

Part of the drive back to the apartment was spent in silence. Then Bruce asked, "I guess you realized I was the one tailing you when you drove by Houseman's warehouse. That guy you hired as a driver surprised me. I couldn't believe he fell in behind me after dropping you at the precinct."

Jim chuckled. "That's Manny Randolf. He's a retired cop and as sharp as a tack. I feel good having him watch my back. I'd like to read him in on what happened tonight; is that okay with you?"

Bruce hesitated. "I'm going to make an executive decision and say yes. My boss might not like it, he's the one who usually calls the shots, but he isn't involved with this case like I am. He only knows what I tell him."

"I trust Manny. He's proven himself a good detective and I'm a pretty good judge of character. And he has innovative ideas!" Jim grinned, thinking of the scenario with making the appointment to see Houseman.

Jim turned in his seat to look at Foster. "What's Houseman's role in all this? I believe it's time for you to tell me what you know. Let's get on the same page."

"It's late, so let's set a time tomorrow to sit down and bring both you and Manny up to date at the same time."

Jim decided he wouldn't tell Beth where he had gone the night before. He didn't intend to share anything about seeing Andy. It was too juicy a bit of news to expect Beth to keep it from Rebecca.

The thought of keeping the information from Dave was quite another thing. His friend had put his career on the line to share the information about Bruce Foster. He went into Andy's office with a cup of coffee and considered the pros and cons. In a short time, Jim decided to share the whole thing with Dave along with swearing him to secrecy.

The two met at a prearranged restaurant; Dave had already arrived.

After being seated, Jim started right in. "Dave, do you remember last Thursday when you told me about Foster; and how you practically had to sign in blood to get the information?"

"Remember it? I can honestly say I've regretted opening my big trap ever since. If it ever came out, I could lose my job!"

"I'm going to ask you to swear that you won't divulge anything I'm about to tell you now." He looked seriously at his friend. "Bruce Foster called me last night and came over to Andy's apartment. We talked a while and swapped information."

To say Dave was surprised was an understatement. "You gotta' be kiddin' me!"

"But I haven't told you the half of it. He took me to a safe house where they had Andy squirreled away. He's alive but pretty beaten up and has a way to go. Foster is going to bring me up to date on what's going on this evening. He's coming over to Andy's apartment and agreed I could bring Manny in on it."

"I'm going to stay as far away as possible to this case because I don't want the FBI to have any idea that I've had anything to do with it. I would appreciate you keeping my name out of it."

Jim agreed and told Dave about the trip he and Beth had made to the Houseman Galleries as well as getting a look at Houseman. He also mentioned how Stevens was helping out by investigating the guy on the Property Desk.

Dave asked, "What's the guy's name on Property?"

Jim thought that was a strange question and he said so.

"My agency has had some flags pop up relating to that department. We considered it might not have anything to do with drugs but perhaps something else." Jim just shook his head. "It seems to me that the government agencies need to start sharing info. Our nation would be much safer and we could be so much further along in stopping some of the plans these drug lords and Jihadists have."

"I quite agree," said Dave. "If both agencies happen to be investigating the same department in a police precinct, we *need* to share information! But I'm not sure that's going to happen considering the way things are now."

Jim spoke with derision, "I'm assuming they're in competition and their goal is to come out on top."

Dave nodded his head, "Afraid so."

The two continued to banter until they had finished their lunch. When they said their goodbyes, Jim offered to call Dave when he knew the outcome for Andy. Later, as Dave mulled over their conversation, he realized that Jim had never answered his question about the man's name in Property. Dave just smiled. *I'm not at all surprised; after all this is the captain I'm dealing with.*

Jim had arranged a time for he and Manny to meet with Bruce Foster the next morning. Beth offered to make lunch before she left to go shopping. It all worked out. Manny came over around 10:30 and the two were talking strategy in the living room when the bell sounded. After Foster came in, Jim introduced Manny and the three men gravitated toward the kitchen.

It pleased Manny to hear he'd passed muster and would be read in on all that was known by the FBI. In the meantime, Jim had asked him to tail Mercer when they were finished. Manny decided to go early in case Mercer went somewhere interesting before work.

He figured that might be the time the man would carry out any clandestine activities.

The gist of what the FBI agent told them was how the agency got wind of some things that alerted them to the possibility of a terrorist attack. They were trying to find out how they got their funding. The agent continued, "A man we've had our eye on by the name of Ali Madur popped up; he's a member of a group of radical thinkers and attends the same mosque we've been watching. When we heard about the Houseman Galleries, we decided to try to plant an agent in the warehouse. It worked for a while but for no reason our man was let go. We heard chatter that indicated there was something big about to happen.

"The FBI was scurrying around for leads, anything of value, when Andy Warren called the office and said he'd like to speak to an agent. He said he suspected a crime was being committed so one of our agents made an appointment with him. During his initial meeting in our offices, he mentioned the Houseman Galleries. I happened to be seated at the next desk and my ears perked up when I heard that name. I immediately called my supervisor in DC and he told me he would take care of it.

"That same afternoon, I was called into the Agent In Charge's office and I was told to handle Mr. Warren's case. I made an appointment with Andy for that day and we went over to his newly leased space. Andy told me he had left instructions with the warehouse to forward any of his deliveries to his new address. I figured someone was going to be in big trouble when they realized the furniture from Paris had been sent to Andy's new shop. When we arrived there, he took me to the back where an antique desk sat."

He added, "Andy had told me that the corner brass decoration on the desk was loose when he uncrated the piece. He said he thought it could be fixed easily and when he got down on the floor to check it out, he saw some fabric wedged near the leg. When he got it out, he found it was a black velvet bag full of large exquisite diamonds."

Foster continued, "We were standing in front of the desk and Andy opened the top drawer and pulled out the black bag, handing it over to me. It was full of diamonds and I figured they were worth millions. It dawned on me this was the *funding* source and they would do whatever it took to get those diamonds back. I told Andy to be very careful. I also called DC to see what they wanted me to do with the diamonds and I was told to put them in the Agency vault immediately.

"That same night, we got a call from our snitch near Houseman's warehouse telling us that a van had pulled out in a hurry and he'd tail it as far as he could without being seen. He turned a corner in time to see the van slow down and something was pushed out of the back door; it looked like a body. He called 9-1-1 immediately and our guys took it from there."

The two sat there digesting what had been divulged by Foster. Jim's mind was in overdrive. What else could go wrong?

His phone rang.

21.
The Unexpected

Beth was browsing in a store when her cell rang. She stepped to a quieter area to take the call. The caller said, "Beth? It's Rebecca. Help m..." The call ended. Beth was frantic and called Rebecca back, but didn't receive an answer. She then called Jim.

"Jim, I'm going over to Rebecca's as soon as I can catch a cab. Will you meet me there?" She then related the strange call.

Jim and Manny were already there when Beth's cab pulled up. There were several police cars parked on the circle, and Manny managed to find out they had responded to a 9-1-1 call from Rebecca's apartment. He also found out from one of his acquaintances on the force that her apartment was being robbed when she walked in on them. They roughed her up a bit, questioning her about some diamonds and knocked her to the floor. She passed out and they got out of there. No one at the building had seen anything.

When Manny received an okay for them to go in, Beth rushed ahead. She halted as the elevator opened and a stretcher was rolled out with Rebecca on it! An oxygen mask was affixed to her pale face. Beth announced she would be going to the hospital in the ambulance with the young woman. When the EMT's balked, Beth forced her way in while telling them Rebecca just found out she was pregnant. She then called Dr. Randall, asking her to meet them at Bellevue. Randall ordered the crew to take her to a room on the obstetrics floor. She wanted her to have the best pre-natal care.

After she had an opportunity to examine her, Dr. Randall came into the waiting room and got Beth. She asked her to follow her to an office where she explained Rebecca's condition. "We're very thankful that the baby's okay. *Mama* has some bad bruises and is naturally scared to death. She keeps mumbling that the same thing happened to her boyfriend; and now her."

Beth's heart of compassion took over. "She can come stay with us. And I'll be glad to stay with her tonight if you think I should."

"I believe if you stayed for awhile, assuring her everything is okay, it would be alright for you to leave when she goes to sleep. There'll be a security guard on the floor who has specifically been made aware of the patient's situation; he'll be watching her room."

Beth sighed with relief. She couldn't imagine the nightmare Rebecca had just been through. "When will she be released, doctor?"

"I'd like to keep her another day, to make sure all is well. Then I'll release her."

Jim and Manny were waiting at the ER entrance. They relayed that Rebecca's apartment had been torn apart like Andy's. They were relieved that Rebecca had the presence of mind to call 9-1-1 before she called Beth.

Around 3 p.m. the next day, Manny parked around the corner from Mercer's house. He dreaded this part of the job but someone had to do it. He sat for 45 minutes before the man left. Manny was about a half block away. When the man turned right at a light, Manny took his time following him and fell in behind, with a car between them. He thought it unlikely Mercer would ever be able to pick up his tail now.

Mercer drove to a mosque on a side street. Manny found a place about a block away and got out of his car. He sauntered past the mosque without looking right nor left; just an ordinary pedestrian. He turned the corner and saw an alley that backed up to the mosque. He considered going back to his car and cutting through the alley. Just then, the back door of the mosque opened and two men followed Mercer out. They were discussing something volatile and Manny could discern Mercer wasn't a bit happy by his raised voice. He only caught an occasional word. . ."nothing. . .know. . .ambulance."

Manny decided to return to his car and be ready to continue tailing Mercer. He followed him surreptitiously to the galleries. Mercer parked in the back and entered the rear door.

The ex-cop decided to drop in and talk with the receptionist again, but she was on a break. *Not supposed to happen,* thought Manny. He left and returned to Andy's apartment to give Jim an update. They both surmised the conversation overheard was probably about Rebecca.

Foster was out front as agreed. The two drove the distance to the safe house and discussed what had happened to Rebecca.

"If he's able, I think we need to take Andy to the hospital. He'll have my head if he finds out we kept it from him," Jim reasoned.

"How in the world is that beat-up patient going to get into the hospital without being detected in case someone is watching?"

Jim thought. "I think he should go in as a patient! We roll him into ER on a stretcher, switch him to a wheel chair and take him up to Rebecca's room."

After some thought, Foster agreed. "Let's talk to Mandy and ask her what she thinks."

The two made their way to the second floor and saw the young nurse sitting at her desk. She brightened when she saw them.

"I'm so glad you came! Did Dr. Keel call you about Andy's improvement today?"

"No," barked the irritated Foster. "I was supposed to hear the minute there *was* any improvement."

"Dr. Keel probably hasn't had a chance to call you as he's been awfully busy today. This morning he checked the patient and left here on the fly." She looked at him cautiously, "Do you want me to call him?"

"No. I guess we'll just take a look ourselves." With that the two men turned and walked into Andy's room. He was sitting up in bed, watching TV and had a cold drink in his hand. The IV bag was gone.

"Hi," he said, "I was wondering if you two would show up today." He grinned, "Do you think you could order me a steak, medium rare, and a baked potato?"

Jim just smiled. Andy was back.

Foster approached the bed and carefully asked, "How're you feeling?"

"Great. I wondered when I was going to get out of this place?"

"Would you like to take a ride with us tonight?"

Andy was surprised. "Are you kidding? I'd like to see anything but these four walls." He looked at the two cautiously. "What have you got in mind?"

Foster held up his hands. "We don't go anywhere until Mandy gives us the okay, so let me go out and ask her." He turned on his heel and left the room. He explained the whole plan to Mandy, she called Dr. Keel, and Keel gave the okay.

As the three left, Andy was propped up in the back seat with a pillow. He looked a little pale and Jim realized that this little bit of activity had taken its toll on him.

During their ride to the hospital, Jim gently explained that

Rebecca had been hurt when she surprised two thieves in her apartment.

Andy was alarmed. "What happened, and how badly was she hurt?" His concern showed in his voice.

"I think they were as surprised as she was, and just lashed out. We're glad it didn't turn out more serious."

Jim chimed in. "She was taken to the hospital to make sure nothing was broken and to keep her under observation overnight."

Andy moaned. "It's all my fault! Those lousy creeps didn't need to hurt her. I'm sure they were looking for the diamonds and she doesn't even know about them."

"Which probably saved her. When they questioned her, they obviously thought she was telling the truth."

Jim shot Bruce a look telling him to back off. He knew Andy and more information would just multiply his fears. Bruce got the message and changed the subject.

When their car pulled into the ER receiving dock, an agent dressed in scrubs was waiting. He and Foster carefully got Andy out of the car and transferred him to a stretcher and a blanket was thrown over him. They walked to the elevator like they belonged there. Bruce pressed the next floor, got out and they transferred Andy to a waiting wheelchair, got back on and rose to the fourth floor.

The elevator opened and Andy observed the sign that said "Obstetrics". He thought, *I guess this is a great place to stash a serious witness.*

Rebecca was sound asleep; the room was dark except for the night-light in the bathroom. One side of her face was beginning to turn colors, but she still looked beautiful. Andy gazed at her from the doorway. He started rolling himself into the room and Jim put a restraining hand on his shoulder. He whispered in his ear, "Don't wake her, they want her to sleep." Andy nodded.

He rolled back out of the room which surprised Jim; he thought Andy would want to stay longer. Andy motioned Jim to lean down and whispered, "I want to stand by her bed. I won't wake her, I promise. I just need to be close to her."

Jim agreed and they wheeled Andy in close to the bed. With effort he rose to his feet. He stood there gazing at his beautiful angel. He gently touched her hand, and her eyelids fluttered. He immediately removed his hand and sat down. She closed her eyes.

After Jim had wheeled him out, he told Bruce to make arrangements for them to leave by the ER entrance. When he turned around, he saw Andy reading Rebecca's chart clipped at the side of her door. Jim's heart sank.

On the way to the car, Andy was very quiet. They started their trip back to the safe house and he mumbled, "Promise me you two will find out who did this to her and give them a little of their own medicine."

They both chimed in, "You got it. We're on it."

When the threesome got Andy up the stairs and into his room, Bruce went out to talk with Mandy. When Jim and Andy were alone, Andy said, "She's pregnant, isn't she?

Jim just nodded. "I don't have many details; Beth does. I know she didn't want you to know; she didn't want you to think she was out to trap you."

Andy turned his head to the wall and Jim patted him, saying his goodbye.

When Jim let himself into the apartment, his mind was racing and he decided to have a drink to relax. He knew he couldn't sleep now!

If ever there was a time when he wanted to share something with Beth, it was now. He needed to think this one through before they told Rebecca Andy was alive.

22.
Plans

Beth went to the hospital to help Rebecca check out Friday morning. The young woman had just been released and called Beth immediately. Rebecca agreed to stay with the Redmons until her apartment was put back in order. They stopped at her apartment and she packed a bag. When the cab deposited the two women at Andy's, they spent the morning rehashing the nightmare Rebecca had just experienced and she told Beth about her dream of seeing Andy. While she rested, Beth went grocery shopping.

The four men met at Andy's apartment the following afternoon. Jim felt they needed to all be privy to the same information. He started the conversation, "We know someone is desperate to find those diamonds and we need to find out why. In my imagination after seeing those guys at the mosque, I think it's got to be for the funding of some kind of attack. I understand those stones are worth millions."

Bruce told the others what the FBI already knew about their friend. "Andy suspected something wasn't kosher long before he found the diamonds. In looking back, he was more analytical when he thought about his relationship with Houseman. He even thought that maybe this wasn't the first time the man had used him as a mule. He said Houseman was using a particular antique store in Paris and made sure there were some lucrative deals for Andy when he was in the country. Ironically the pieces were always purchased at the same antique store. We have our people watching the place."

Bruce turned to Stevens, "I understand you were going to check on the security tapes near the galleries. Did you see anything of interest?"

"Not really, mainly customers going in and out; the camera that covers the back is out of order."

Manny shared the outcome of his tail on Mercer. Stevens

seemed surprised the man went to the mosque and later was seen with the two men suspected of roughing Rebecca up. "There's a reasonable clue that supports Jim's *imagination* that it may have something to do with an attack...a terrorist attack. I think I'll continue to follow Mercer."

Only one person differed and Stevens spoke up, "I believe it would be more profitable to us if you followed Lockman."

Jim asked, "Is there any way we can find out who 'Lockman' is? He was one of the voices on Andy's cell and he became more agitated with each call."

Bruce offered, "I can find out what we know already. I know he works in the warehouse; I'll go make a call now." He ducked into the kitchen.

Bob Stevens spoke up, "It's well known that the mosque Mercer went to the other day has some radical thinkers. We've been keeping a watch on the place just because my *gut* says we should. Lots of activity recently." He turned to Jim, "I agree with you, they're getting ready for something."

Bruce walked back into the room, overhearing the last comment. "And that makes it more imperative to get some answers soon and break this cell wide open before an attack takes place."

"What did you find out about Lockman?"

"He's the warehouse manager. We had an agent planted there but they let him go because we think they didn't want any outside eyes on what was going on. Initially he was hired for a large shipment coming in, and since he proved himself a hard worker they let him stay on a little longer. Before he left, he said he overheard one phone conversation where Lockman used Houseman's name. He was obviously taking some kind of instructions."

"Did he give you any useful information while he was there?" Stevens was very interested.

"He said all three warehouse workers were middle eastern men; all tight as a knot. They were definitely not friendly. And he said Houseman never came to the warehouse, that he was aware of. The boss was Lockman."

Jim spoke, "I agree with Bob; Manny follows Lockman instead."

"I'll start tomorrow when he gets off work," said Manny. He turned to Bruce, "Does your agency by any chance know where he lives?"

"I'll make another call before we leave here and give you all that we've learned about our Mr. Lockman."

Manny found out where Lockman lived and decided to head that way after the warehouse closed, picking him up on his way home. The plan worked well. Manny pulled out of a gas station when he saw Lockman's car pass. He followed him to his neighborhood and decided to pass on by when the man turned. Manny did a U-turn up the street and doubled back.

Lockman parked in the driveway and let himself into the front door. Manny parked on the street a few doors down and waited. In about thirty minutes, another car pulled up and parked out front. Two men got out, dressed in jeans and parkas, and disappeared into the house. Manny took a picture of the two men and their car with his cell. He made a notation of the license plate number. Before long, a pickup drove up and parked in the driveway. One man ran for the door before Manny could get a picture of him. After thinking about it, he decided to call Jim and let him know what was going on.

"Jim, it's Manny. Looks like a meeting is going on at Lockman's house. I've counted three visitors plus Lockman. I plan to stay and see if I can tail one of them."

"I'll use your truck and see if I can give you a hand. Give me the address again."

He told Jim to park around the next corner. He'd call him when someone was leaving so he could tail him.

It was cold sitting in that drafty old truck. Jim turned on the engine every fifteen minutes to take the chill off. An hour had passed when his cell rang.

"Yo."

"Someone is leaving and he's getting into a blue pickup, headed your way."

"Got it," said Jim. He waited for the truck to pass. He approached the corner and fell in behind, leaving about a block between the two vehicles. The truck pulled into a convenience store and the young man got out. Jim could see through the window and the guy didn't appear to be middle Eastern. He slowly pulled around the corner hoping the man was headed in the same direction. It worked because eventually the blue pickup passed him.

As Jim followed the truck, he realized the man wasn't going into Manhattan. He drove to a residential neighborhood and pulled into a drive, jumped out of his truck and walked down the street. Jim realized he was walking toward the subway entrance they had passed earlier. *Where is he headed?* he said to himself.

Jim decided to call Manny, then Bruce. He told Manny what had happened.

"I'll call Stevens and ask him to check out who owns the truck and anything relevant. In the meantime, this meeting is still going on and I believe I'll only wait another thirty minutes, then I'm outta' here."

Jim called Foster's cell and told him what was happening. "We've got to find out where this guy works so Manny's going to see if he can find out who owns the truck." He sent all the pictures Manny had sent.

Foster was surprised. He already knew about Lockman's house and his clandestine meetings but as yet never had the men followed. All of them had been seen at the mosque. He also had all the license numbers and descriptions. Jim sensed something wasn't quite right.

With a caustic tone, Jim said, "You already know most of this, don't you Bruce?"

Bruce knew the PI was irritated and tried to appease him. "I never thought it was important."

"Oh come on. *Everything* we learn about this case is important. It makes me mad to think you allowed Manny to hang out in front of Lockman's when you knew the answers to our questions." He paused, "I wonder how much you haven't told me."

"I swear, I've told you all I'm permitted."

"Umm. I guess I'll have to accept that," said Jim.

He sure is sharper than I gave him credit, thought Foster.

Back at the apartment, the tired PI sat back in the comfortable chair and mulled over all they knew up to this point. He definitely wasn't happy that Bruce Foster held back some information which could have saved them a heap of time, and save both he and Manny from sitting in front of Lockman's house in the cold. Foster *should* have told them.

Before Manny left, the meeting ended and the men exited the house. He followed their car to a run-down apartment building. They disappeared inside and Manny headed for Jim's.

"Do you ever get over the frustration of having to sit around and wait; especially in the cold?" complained Manny.

"I'm with you on that one," replied Jim. He decided then and there not to tell Manny what he had just learned from Foster. He didn't want a firestorm. "Once we get a name, I hope Foster can find out where he works."

While the two men were talking, Stevens called. "I got the name of the owner of that truck. His name is Sven Abadi and he's squeaky clean. He's 24 years old and lives with his father. His parents are separated or divorced."

"That's a start," said Jim." It'd be interesting to find out something about him, especially his political leaning."

"I'll see what I can find out," offered Stevens.

When he got off the phone, Jim filled Manny in and they decided to find out what high school he'd attended and check out the year book.

Jim called Stephens back. "You wouldn't happen to know what high school Abadi attended, would you? We're thinking about checking out the year books to see what we can learn." Stevens promised to check and call them right back. As promised, he had the information for them in twenty minutes.

"Good," declared Jim. "We'll start with that on Monday morning." Manny left with a promise to pick up Jim at 9 a.m. on Monday morning; he had the weekend off!

23.
The Other Side

Fred Houseman sat at his expensive antique desk in the library. His guest was nervously tapping his foot, squirming in his chair. It looked like he was on the hot seat, which he was.

"What do you *mean* 'she didn't know anything'? Someone has to know what happened to those stones! And if she's Warren's girlfriend, she's the most likely one to have that information." Houseman's anger was evident.

"We were going to try to squeeze more out of her, but she fainted before we could. We had just finished searching her apartment when she returned and it caught us by surprise. She screamed and we were afraid someone had heard her. We quickly dragged her into the apartment and Butch smacked her across the face to quiet her down. He then told her to tell us where the diamonds were, but she screamed 'No. No, don't hit me again. I don't know anything about any diamonds!' Butch grabbed her and started roughing her up. She was terrified and just fainted. I honestly don't think she knows anything."

"Are you sure you two did a thorough search?"

"Yes. We did as thorough a search as we did at Warren's apartment. If those stones are in that apartment, it'd take a scent on them and a police dog to find them."

The older man looked beyond his guest as if looking at a scene far away. He quietly spoke, as if to himself, "I wonder if the stones were ever in the piece? We expertly questioned Warren and he didn't know what we were talking about. My men held nothing back in trying to coerce him to talk; in fact they went too far and killed him."

The man sitting before him remained silent. He knew the boss was thinking out loud and a reply wasn't expected.

"Zero hour is in two weeks and there is *no* room for error. Our supplier is getting antsy and it isn't safe to string him along." With a wave of his hand, he said, "I need to think about this further. This is as big as 9/11!" He slowly came to his feet. "You are dismissed," he said, and turned his back to the man.

The visitor quickly got up and headed for the door. Before he could turn the knob, Houseman said, "Tell Ali Madur I want to see him ASAP."

"Yes sir." And he was gone and glad of it.

Ali Madur called Houseman and made arrangements to go to the mansion the following morning. After he hung up, Houseman locked the study door and walked to the bookcase. He pressed a lever under the third shelf and the bookcase swung open. There was a small neat, compact room that held a desk, computer, and phone. He sat down and placed a call to the antique store in Paris.

"Pierre, this is Fred Houseman. We did not receive our shipment here. I thought it may be a problem with the man who made the purchase of the desk at your shop. Regardless, after expert questioning he didn't seem to know what we were talking about. Sadly, he is no longer with us. The shipment you sent has disappeared so tell me exactly what you did from the moment you hid the diamonds until it was picked up for delivery."

The Frenchman relayed all the steps covered before the boat sailed. He was as perplexed as Houseman *and* a bit nervous. It could become dangerous for him if Houseman thought he was behind the disappearance of the diamonds. "Do you think they could have been stolen from the container?"

"I very much doubt it. It makes me nervous about our deadline."

Houseman was more than concerned about the problem. He decided to go with his decision to talk with Madur about it.

The next morning, Ali Madur was shown into the library. Ali was a cocky Arab with too much American influence in him as far as Houseman was concerned. But Ali was indispensible and for that reason Houseman was not willing to get rid of him. . . yet.

"I have some sensitive questions for you, Ali. As you know, we still don't know where our diamonds are but I've made some phone calls and we're still hopeful we can retrieve them. Our time-schedule is looming and I need to get my hands on some explosives, for free." He looked at the young man to see his reaction but the young man sat with no expression on his face, which infuriated Houseman because he couldn't read him. He continued, "Do we have any brothers working a construction site in or around New York?"

Ali seemed to be turning the question around in his mind. "What you really mean is can we steal some explosives to replace the ones we were going to buy?"

The man had concisely read the situation perfectly. Houseman's face turned red. "Yes, that's what I mean," he barked. "If we hope to accomplish our goal, we need explosives right away; our date is in two weeks." He banged his fist on the desk in frustration.

"What are you going to do about the source you promised to buy them from?"

"I'll worry about that," he retorted. "You just rustle the bushes and find me some free explosives, and I'll make it worth your while." He read the avaricious young man perfectly. It bothered Houseman that this guy wasn't as patriotic to their cause as he would like. The American greed had wormed its way into the man's way of thinking. But no mind, he'd take care of it *after* they had achieved their objective.

"I have some ideas," offered Ali. "I'll get on it right away."

Houseman was pleased, "Good, I look forward to hearing from you soon."

The next phone call Fred Houseman made was to the warehouse where he talked with Lockman. "This is way too sensitive to talk about over the phone. Can we meet in my office in about an hour?"

"I'll be there," responded Lockman.

When the two met, Houseman questioned the man about the search that was made at Warren's new shop.

"A couple of our men went over and let themselves in. They found the shipping crate in the back of the building and it looked like the desk had been removed and then put back into the crate. We carefully removed the brass leaf on each leg. They all came up empty with no sign of any diamonds. We checked around the place and there wasn't anything to look *into*. There wasn't even a desk or phone in the place. Obviously Warren hadn't moved in yet. There was also a prepared bill of lading laying on top for someone to pick up and deliver the piece to another place."

This lined up with what they got out of Warren. He said he didn't find any diamonds. In fact, he acted like he didn't know what they were talking about. The men had ways of getting information but nothing yielded a different story than Warren told in the beginning. Now Warren was dead.

Madur made some calls and found out there were two friends working on a construction site on the outskirts of Manhattan. They were tearing down a building and using some dynamite. They could get their hands on some, but it would be tricky. The minute it was discovered, the authorities would be called in and he figured they didn't need that kind of trouble. They were going to call Madur back as soon as they had a workable plan. He told them that their time frame was creeping up and he needed an answer soon.

Ali called Houseman and reported his conversation. He expected to hear back within a day or so and Houseman was somewhat relieved.

24.
School Days

On Monday morning, Jim jumped into Manny's car and they took off for the high school.

"Before you came, I called the school and made an appointment with the principal. He's expecting us and will have several yearbooks for us to look through. He seemed like a nice man and wants to be helpful," said Jim.

"I put the school into my GPS so we should be there in short order. I'm curious, are we supposed to be with the Police Department? I know he can't give any information about a student to just anybody who walks in off the street."

"I told him I was a detective and a police officer would be accompanying me; meaning YOU, with your bogus ID. There shouldn't be any problem. He may not even ask to see it." Jim seemed to change gears and quipped, "Have you ever had to go to a school and check out old yearbooks before?"

"Once I went with a Juvenile Court-appointed psychologist. It probably will be easier today since we won't be checking medical and counseling records. Piece-a-cake."

The rest of the trip the two men planned some of their questions. They felt prepared when they met the principal. After the initial introductions, the three moved into Mr. Sloan's office and sat at a conference table. There were three yearbooks already on the table.

"If you have need of any information, I'll be happy to answer what I can." Sloan offered.

"We'll just start looking through the yearbooks and if we need some information, we'll be sure to ask."

The two friends started looking at different books. Quickly Manny found Abadi's picture in the sophomore section. "Here he is as a sophomore," he said to Jim, and passed the book over. The two examined the picture of a boy with light brown hair and the palest blue eyes he'd ever seen! What was startling was his olive complexion.

"Here he is in the senior section of graduates," mentioned Jim. He showed the picture to Manny. "He looks much more mature. I'm going to check to see if he was active in school activities as a senior."

They called Mr. Sloan over and asked him if he had been at the school when Sven had attended there.

"When I started here, he was a freshman but I didn't have any interaction with the boy in his freshman or sophomore years. When he was a junior, he had some run-ins with other boys. It doesn't take much to become the one everyone is anxious to pick on. By his last name the boys knew Abadi was of middle-eastern dissent and I heard him called a "rag head", among other things. He didn't much like that and started swinging, which ended up by him being sent to my office. A couple weeks later, I had to call his father after a similar incident and discovered that Mr. Abadi was definitely not going to get involved. I guess the *sticks and stones* saying didn't apply to Sven's situation. I wondered if his father was even going to talk to him about using fist-fights to resolve problems. It looked like I was wrong, because the young man seemed to become very amiable and wasn't easily baited afterward. I was happily relieved that it all worked out."

"Can you give us any information about his parents? I know he lives with his father, but what can you tell me about his mother?" asked Jim.

"His mother is of Norwegian descent. I understand she left her husband and son when he just started elementary school. And that's about all I know about her."

Manny interjected, "Did Abadi have any close friends at school?"

"He did have a girlfriend but it ended after a few months. Her name was Angela Mesconi and I understand her father put a stop to the relationship."

"I know it's been a few years, but would you happen to know how we could get in touch with Angela?" asked Jim.

"That's one question the FBI didn't ask me," he said thoughtfully. "Her dad used to have a Mom-n-Pop grocery called 'Mesconi's'. I've never been there so don't know where it's located." Sloan seemed thoughtful. "If that doesn't help, we can always check with the alumni organization. They stay pretty active until a student's ten year reunion."

Sloan had just dropped a bomb about the FBI, but he recovered without a hitch. Jim asked, "I see where he was on the wrestling team his junior and senior year. Is the same wrestling coach still at this school?"

"Why yes, he is. I'll call him to the office; he's on a break now."

Soon the wrestling coach appeared at the office door. "You wanted to see me, Mr. Sloan?"

"Yes, come in Arnold. These two men are with the Police Dept. and would like some information about Sven Abadi. Would you answer some questions for them?"

The question and answer session with Coach Arnold didn't offer much personal information about Abadi. "I felt like Abadi was too lanky to be any good at the sport, and I was right."

Manny had managed to locate the Mesconi grocery store on his cell and the two men headed over there. On their drive over, the two sleuths talked about Sloan's saying the FBI had been there. Jim just shook his head; he was learning more and more about what Foster *had not* thought to share with them.

The two men entered a typical small neighborhood grocery store. It wasn't large and didn't have an abundance of products on its shelves. When they entered, a young woman was waiting on a customer. They immediately recognized Angela from her yearbook picture. They waited for her to finish.

"May I help you?" she asked.

He stepped up to the counter while Manny hung back and checked out the latest magazine covers. "Yes, you may. My name is Jim Redmon and if I may I'd like to ask you some questions."

"What about?" she asked suspiciously.

"I'm trying to locate a young man named Sven Abadi. According to Mr. Sloan at the high school, I understand you two dated while you were in high school."

The girl looked around frantically, to make sure no one overheard their conversation. They were alone. She answered quietly, "That's right. We dated a short time so I don't know what I can tell you about him." She was definitely on the defensive and ready for these two men to get lost.

"He's not in trouble. It's just a legal situation and we need to try to get some information. Is there some place we can go to talk privately?"

Once again, she looked around the store. When satisfied no one else was there, she said, "My sister will be here soon because I'm due for a break. There's a coffee shop a couple of blocks down and I'll answer your questions there." The bell rang and another customer entered as they left.

The coffee shop was mediocre, at best. The two men chose a booth near the back and waited while sipping a cup of coffee. Jim declared, "If the owner of this shop would sell his secret for making coffee, he'd be rich." Manny nodded in agreement.

The two continued with small talk until Angela Mesconi came in. She seemed relieved they were seated in the back. This was, after all, her neighborhood with people who knew her.

Jim realized they needed to make this a quick visit. He started by offering her a cup of coffee, which he ordered. She seemed to relax a bit and they remarked how great the coffee was and their thinking that the recipe could make the owner rich.

She chuckled and said, "It's not the first time that's been suggested."

Jim decided to lie a bit and said, "Miss Mesconi, may I call you Angela?" She nodded. "We work for a lawyer trying to find Sven Abadi's mother. You see, she stands to receive quite a nice inheritance but no one seems to know how to contact her. Would you know anything that might help us?"

The girl was surprised. This was the last thing she expected to hear from these two men. To her, they looked like cops, but she assumed that was exactly the type a lawyer would hire to locate a missing person.

She spoke with a low voice, "I don't know if you are aware of this, but Sven and I didn't date long. When my father realized he was a Muslim, he forbid me from seeing him. My father's a strong Catholic with old-fashioned ideas."

Jim smiled. "And I have a daughter about your age and know full well that if I said she couldn't see a guy any more, she'd show me!"

Angela blushed. "Well, I did see him a while longer. It was exciting sneaking around, but it didn't last long." She paused as if trying to decide how much more to reveal.

Jim reached over and patted her hand. "It's okay. We're not the *dating police.* We certainly have nothing to gain by telling your father you talked to us. We just want to know if Sven may have confided in you enough to share about his family."

Whatever Jim said, the dam was released and Angela poured out all she knew. She seemed relieved to share with someone.

The pretty young woman clasped her cup between her hands.

"When we first started dating, Sven seemed interested in hearing about the relationship I had with my mother. He'd ask the strangest questions, like, 'Did your mother read to you?' He also wanted to know if my mother was proud when I did good in school?" She paused. "Stuff like that. When I asked him why he wanted to know, he said his mother had left when he was just starting school. He said he *thought* she loved him and my heart ached for him because he didn't seem to know." The young woman looked wistful.

She continued, "I'm a typical female and I wanted more details. When he was in the mood, he'd tell me more stuff. For instance, I put two and two together and realized his father was mean to his mother. Sven said she cried a lot."

Jim gently asked her, "Did his father worship anywhere?"

"His father was very active in the local mosque. And he was doing a good job instructing Sven in the Muslim faith, too! Sven shared with me that he was beginning to see the truth in what his father believed and started hinting that we should both seriously investigate the faith. That scared me and I started having doubts about him." The young woman seemed to reach back in her memory. "Once his father told him that his mother had refused to behave like a good Muslim woman and he wouldn't tolerate it! Things went downhill for her from then on. He made life miserable for her but only once did Sven witness his father hitting her. I guess he broke her arm because they had to take her to the emergency room. He shared with me how much it scared him; and it also made him afraid of his father."

Jim probed, "Did Sven tell you when that happened?"

"It happened just before his mother left, so I guess it was around the time he started school."

"Did Sven ever learn where his mother went?" Manny asked.

"He guessed she might have gone back to her family. They lived in Wisconsin and she had told Sven how she longed to go back to visit them on their farm. She would love to take Sven with her, but when he mentioned it to his father, World War III broke out. He said he could hear his mother crying and his father raging at her and threatening her. By the sounds he heard, he thought his father had beaten her. He remembers cowering in bed frantic he would be next. The next morning, he said his mother had disappeared."

"Did he ever ask his father where his mother had gone?"

"He said his mother didn't love them anymore and had left. He said he didn't know where she had gone, and he forbid Sven from talking about her ever again."

Jim had to bring sense to his questioning, and asked. "Too bad Sven didn't know where in Wisconsin his grandparent's farm was. That sure would help us."

"I do remember him saying it was near the city of York, Wisconsin. I recall the name because it reminded me of New York."

Jim thought, *bingo.*

The conversation in the coffee shop came to a close and Jim thanked Angela profusely for the information. He cautioned the girl not to divulge anything about their visit to anyone, particularly Sven, *if* she saw him again. "No use in getting his hopes up only to be dashed," he added. She nodded with a knowing, concerned look.

25.
Loose Ends

As soon as Jim got into the car, he called Bruce Foster. "We talked with the principal this morning and he gave us the name of the girl Abadi dated in high school. It was a very informative visit."

Foster mused, *Too bad Jim Redmon wouldn't be interested in joining the FBI; he's way too sharp to be a po-dunk detective in a little town in Tennessee.* "What's her name?"

"Angela Mesconi, and I promised her father would never find out we had questioned her, or that she had given us any information about Abadi. We told her we were investigators looking for Mrs. Abadi regarding a sizable inheritance." Jim continued, "One gold nugget she remembered was Sven saying his mother was from a farm near York, Wisconsin. Could you find out the mother's full name on a marriage license or when she enrolled Sven in kindergarten?"

"Sure," responded Bruce. "I'll get right on it. You know, a birth certificate has a lot more information and might be quicker to find. In the meantime, I'll have our Madison office put on stand-by."

"There's hope for you yet, Foster. You're beginning to think like me!"

Foster chuckled. "Yeah, yeah. Seriously, I'll start searching for records for the woman's full name. I'll call you when I have something. I have this uneasy feeling in my gut we're short on time and we need to look under every rock. . .now!"

"Well, you guys have a ton more resources than we do." He chuckled, "I knew you were good for *some*thing, Foster."

It didn't take the FBI long to find Sven's birth records. He was born in New York at the famous Bellevue Hospital. His mother's full name was Katarina Knutzen, age 21, and she was from York, Wisconsin. The new father was listed as Ahmed Abadi, age 29. He was born in Brooklyn, New York. From there, they checked marriage certificates and saw that the couple married six months before their baby was born.

Bruce Foster called his liaison in Madison. They discussed a plan of action and a team was dispatched to York within the hour. Bruce called Redmon and told him what was in the works. Needless to say, Jim would have liked to be in on the questioning of Katarina Knutzen Abadi.

The neat farmhouse was located about five hundred yards from the road. The agents could tell it was a prosperous farm by the neatness of the grounds and the many outbuildings. They drove up the long driveway and stepped out of their SUV. As they approached the door, it opened and a young woman stepped out onto the porch. She must have been a real beauty when Abadi met her."

"I felt like someone would come knocking on the door with bad news sooner than later," she said with resignation.

With raised eyebrows, Matt Singleton said, "Pardon me?"

"You're with the police or sheriff's department, aren't you?" she said.

Singleton reached for his badge and opened it for the woman to see. "No ma'am, we're from the FBI." The woman blanched, taking a step back.

'Are you Katarina Abadi?" he asked.

She nodded, with frightened eyes. "Yes. I'm Katarina." She clasped her sweater tightly around her. "Has something happened to my son?"

"No ma'am. We just need to ask you some questions. Would it be alright for us to come in out of the cold?"

She glanced around and said, "Alright. But you'll have to leave if my father comes in. He wants me to forget I ever lived in New York!"

The two agents followed her into the old-fashioned parlor off the front hall. Matt Singleton introduced his partner, slipped his jacket off, and sat gingerly on the sofa. (His partner surreptitiously clicked on his recorder.) "We would like to know if you have any information about your husband's politics? We have reason to believe he is involved with a radical group in New York City."

"Oh my God, I was afraid that would happen."

"Could you elaborate, Mrs. Abadi."

The woman sighed and began to tell a story of a young couple meeting in New York City, falling in love, and marrying after learning she was pregnant. They had a little boy and she named him Sven, after her father. It was the first time she had ever seen her husband that upset. He was livid when she told him she had named the child after her father. She felt her husband would get over his initial anger, but he proved her wrong. Regardless, her little boy was the light of her eye and she nourished him in body, mind, and spirit.

"When Ahmed discovered I was teaching the boy why we celebrated Christmas, he went into a rage. It frightened me so much that I gathered my three year old in my arms and ran for the bathroom, locking the door. This infuriated him so much that he kicked the door in. It was the first beating he had given me.

"From then on, Ahmed became fanatical about his Muslim faith; which surprised me because there wasn't even any mention of it before we married. He then refused for me to even sing little songs to our son, like *Jesus Loves Me*. I became more and more frightened of this man who was supposed to be my loving husband. He became more hateful toward our country, and I could see what was happening. The mosque he attended was a hate-mongering place and he became more and more hard to live with."

The woman had tears running down her cheeks as she continued. "It all came to a head when Sven was five years old; I had just enrolled him in school that day. I was telling him about his grandparents and about this farm. He asked if we could go visit them and I told him of course, knowing full well Ahmed would never permit it. In all his innocence, Sven told his father about going to visit his grandparent's farm with mommy and it sent Ahmed into the worst rage I'd ever seen. It was so frightening, I feared for my life and that of my child."

Katarina shuddered when she related the following. "He was ranting and raving and told me I had to leave, without our son, and if I didn't he would kill both of us! Sven was screaming with fright and Ahmed picked him up and put him in his room. Than he threw a few of my things into a suitcase and pushed me out of the apartment, locking the door behind me. I was too afraid to knock on the door and plead with him." She hung her head in shame. "A local church helped me with bus fare to Wisconsin, and I came home." She was wiping her eyes with her sweater, bereft. It had happened years before but it was as fresh as if it had happened last week. "I don't even have a picture of my dear little boy."

"Mrs. Abadi, I think you did the only thing you could do. I just want to make you aware that Mr. Abadi has been indoctrinating Sven with his political views. From what we understand, your son wasn't that involved while he was in high school, but since then, we can only guess. He may be broaching a *no return* path in his life."

Katarina's blue eyes grew large with fright. "I *must* see my son once more before he gets sucked into his father's fanatical ways. It may be too late, but I need to tell him the truth about why I left him!"

The agent promised to see what he could do. But he cautioned her not to take things into her own hands. A serious investigation was going on and anything could tip the scales. She promised to wait for them to contact her within the week.

26.
Wisconsin to New York

When Bruce Foster reported the results of the interview with Katarina Abadi, Jim was full of questions *and* suggestions.

"Hold on a minute, Jim. I'm coming right over and will have a copy of the interview with Mrs. Abadi. That ought to satisfy your first fifty questions. Then I'm open to any suggestions you may want to make after that."

"What time can you be here? I want Manny here, too."

Manny arrived before Foster and the three went into the study to discuss the case. Manny could tell Jim was antsy and wanted to get on with it; forget the niceties. But being the southern gentleman he was, he offered them coffee or a drink. Coffee it was, for all three.

"Okay. Play the recording," said Jim, not beating around the bush.

They listened to the recording from start to finish. All were silent after it was over; everyone deep in thought. Bruce thought he knew what Jim would suggest; he waited to hear it from the man himself.

"How soon can you feds get Katarina here?" said Jim.

"I'm assuming that's what you think should happen, right?" he calmly replied.

"Of course! The sooner the better; her son is key, I can feel it." He jumped up and paced around the room. "We need to find out where he works in Manhattan."

"I have that information," The agent placidly replied. "It's a steak house in Grand Central Station."

With that, Jim dropped into his chair again. "Man, this is getting more and more frightening. If those diamonds were to underwrite an attack, we have to break this up before they find a way to complete their plans."

"Exactly," responded Foster.

Jim composed himself and the other two could almost hear the wheels turning. He slapped his knees and spoke. "When Katarina gets here, we need to ask her to see if she can find out anything from Sven. It may yield nothing, but we have to give her a chance. If we get some good intel, it can only help us." He looked directly at Bruce. "Like I said, how long before we can get Katarina here?"

Foster looked at his watch, "She should be landing at Kennedy within thirty minutes."

Jim looked at Foster with a grin, "You *are* beginning to think like me." He then asked, "Are you going to allow me to sit in on this?"

"It took some persuasive maneuvering but the powers that be finally said yes. I explained to them that we wouldn't even know about Katarina Abadi without you!"

"Way to go, partner." He gave him a fist-bump.

Redmon had more questions. "Where are you taking her when she arrives?"

"It's already arranged, Jim. Our agents will take her to our office directly from the airport. You are invited to be there when we bring her in, but only our agents will be allowed to talk with her." He looked long and hard at Jim. "Do you think you can abide by that rule?"

Jim considered what Bruce was saying to him. Yes, he'd like to have more input with Katarina, but realized he was lucky to be included when they brought her in. He nodded his assent.

Manny just sat there looking back and forth from man to man. To say he was impressed was putting it mildly. He'd been in law enforcement for years and never experienced two lawmen who were so in-tune!

Bruce called his agent on the ground at the airport. "Is the plane on time?" He paused to listen to the man's reply. "We'll be there when you bring her in."

He placed another call and asked if there were eyes on Sven. He replied, "He doesn't get home 'til late, so maybe he's sleeping. Is his father home yet?"

Foster shared with Jim what the agent had told him: "We think the father usually arrives home shortly before Sven goes to work. At least that's what we've observed the few days we've been watching their apartment. So no, there's been no sign of him yet."

Jim considered time constraints and said, "We have to allow Mrs. Abadi a private meeting with her son. She needs time alone with him for obvious reasons. I think it would be great if we could arrange it for tonight when he gets off work. It eliminates making explanations to his father if he arrives home late." He looked to Bruce for his concurrence. "We don't know this guy or if he has a temper. It would be appalling if he flew off the handle and tried to hurt her."

"Good point," Foster agreed. The plan was to have Katarina in an unmarked car at the curb when Sven left work. She would roll down her car window and call out to him asking if she could ask him a question. When he approached, she would get out of the car and meet him face to face. He couldn't fail to notice her sky-blue eyes, just like his, and hopefully there would be a hint of remembrance. Yes, it had been about 19 years, but they were counting on something good to come of this.

After she initially spoke to Sven, she'd ask him if they could talk. If he balked, they had a plan for what she would say. It would be up to him if he'd hear her out; and Jim thought he would.

When Katarina entered the conference room at FBI headquarters, Jim was seated at the table. Bruce rose and greeted her and then introduced himself and his two agents. He then turned to Jim introducing him as their consultant on the case.

Bruce had never met such a lovely woman; Katarina was striking. Her white-blond hair fell to her shoulders, her skin was clear as a baby's, and she wore only a hint of lipstick. She was tall, around five foot eight, with not an ounce of fat on her. He figured she must work on the farm to stay in such good shape.

Katarina was seated and Bruce was going to outline the plan for the evening. "First of all, we want to thank you for your willingness to do this," he said with sincerity. "Did our agents tell you that we're fearful that your son may be involved in a terrorist attack."

"They did tell me it was a serious investigation and not to tell anyone. Knowing his father, I just put two and two together and figured it had to be something like that."

Bruce spoke, "Here's what we plan to do. . ." And he laid out the plan.

"Why do I have to wear a wire?" She asked.

"It's been about nineteen years since you saw your son, Mrs. Abadi." He paused, "Can I call you Katarina?"

"Of course," she said, as she glanced up at him with blue eyes that leveled him.

Bruce continued, "He's been under the influence and discipline of Ahmed Abadi and from what we've learned, he's a rather brutal man."

The woman nodded her head, lifting her eyes with a question. "How do you know that?"

"When we talked with a girl Sven dated in high school, she told us some things he had shared about you and his father. That's why we're hopeful he'll be agreeable to talk with you and we hope will listen to some sense."

"I'll do whatever it takes to try to save my son from this nightmare!"

The next hour the FBI prepared Katarina further for her evening with her son. They even drove her around the area so she'd be familiar with where she was going. Bruce's attention wandered more than once as he interacted with Katarina. Jim could tell he was smitten.

Jim had never inquired about Bruce Foster's personal life. They were so caught up in the case, it never came up. *I notice he isn't wearing a wedding ring; I wonder if he's divorced? If Beth were here, she'd have answers to those questions in record time.*

With several hours free until the meeting with Sven, Bruce took Katarina to her hotel. She went up to her room to freshen up while he waited in the lobby. She came down after a short time and smiled at him when he stood up.

"This is a very nice hotel and I appreciate you taking the time to escort me around until my meeting with Sven." He noticed she had slipped on some heels but still had to look up at him. For some reason it pleased him.

Before Bruce took her to eat, he reminded her that they would have to be back at headquarters in time to get her wire in place and pick up the car. They had dinner at a cozy restaurant and the two enjoyed an evening talking, with not a lull in the conversation. Later, when he had dropped Katarina at her hotel, Bruce reflected on the evening. He found her intelligent *and* beautiful. He thought, *I can't believe I finally met someone that really interests me and she lives in another state!* He sighed.

Katarina had similar thoughts. . .and sighed.

It was around 11 pm and Katarina's loaner was brought around. Even though they had driven her around the area, they had her follow one of their cars so she wouldn't get lost. She hated the wire attached to her chest. The sound of her beating heart was like a kettle drum and she was sure everyone could hear it. She couldn't remember being this nervous in years and in some ways wished it were over. She wondered if she could get Sven to talk with her. Well she'd know shortly, because Sven just walked out the door. She thought, *I'd know him anywhere.* She drank in his appearance and had difficulty reigning in her emotions. She rolled her window down and called out, "Could you please give me some directions?"

"Sure," he answered. As he walked toward her car, she opened the door and walked around the car meeting Sven on the sidewalk. Sven was before her and she looked into his eyes and said, "Sven?"

He was shocked. *No, it can't be. She reminds me of my mother, but so many years have passed and. . .can it be?* He was confused.

"Sven, it's me, your mother. Can we talk?"

"Wha. . .who. . .You can't be." He looked to his right and then his left, as if looking for a place to run. With determination, he managed to calm down.

"Can we take a drive to a place where we can talk in private? I don't want to stand in the street to talk to you about something so important."

The young man seemed to retrieve some of the anger he had felt for years. He yelled, "You think you can walk back into my life after you abandoned me so long ago? No way, lady."

The hurt in her eyes wounded him. He remembered the look; it triggered some memories he didn't want to remember. She looked deep into his eyes and said, "I would have come years ago, but I was afraid for you *and* me. Won't you at least give me a little bit of your time to hear *why* I left you?"

"I already know. Father told me you didn't love us anymore." He looked like a hurt little boy and meekly said, "You didn't even say goodbye!"

Katarina took a risk and stepped close to him, firmly clasping his arms. He started to wrench away from her grasp, but she held him tighter. "Just give me a few minutes of your time. After you've heard what I have to say and you still want to be rid of me, I promise I'll never bother you again."

Sven seemed to quiet down and looked into her eyes. All he saw there was love; the love he so sorely missed for so long. He agreed to get in the car with her, and they slowly pulled away. She reached over and touched his hand, the hand of a man, and she wanted to cry when she thought of the many years she missed holding her little child's hand. She drove to a parking area she had seen when the FBI was showing her the area.

The words tumbled out of Sven before she even turned the engine off. "Tell me now! Why did you leave me? I could hardly believe Father when he said you didn't love us anymore. I knew you didn't love him, I could tell how scared you were of him." He implored, "but I felt like you still loved *me*." The delivery of his words crushed her; he spoke like a child.

Katarina spoke, "Sven, do you remember how angry and volatile your father had become? The night I left he came storming into the room with a malicious look on his face. He was upset because he misunderstood what I had told you earlier that day. He started yelling and it frightened you and you were crying. He picked you up and put you in your room. He was convinced that I was making plans to run off and take you with me. He became so furious that I feared what he would do to me. In fact, he had me by the throat and I thought he was going to strangle me. As I gasped for breath, he eased his hands off and spoke with such vehemence that I trembled with fright. He said if I tried to leave with you, he'd kill me *and* you. He said I could leave without you but if I ever came back or made any trouble for him, I would seal your death." Tears were running down her face as she lived through the misery once again. "Sven, he was so unstable I believed him. He threw some of my clothes in a bag and threw me out of the apartment, locking the door behind me. I was too afraid to knock, beg or plead, so I left. I ran downstairs to Mrs. Jalabi's apartment."

The young man had a look of shock and disbelief on his face. But he knew it was the truth. Whispering, he said, "I believe you; he is so warped; he's capable of anything!"

"Oh Sven, my Sven," she pleaded, "come back to my parent's farm with me. He'll never know where you disappeared to and you'll be welcomed by my family."

His eyes took on a serious look. "I can't. I have some important plans in the works,"

Katarina looked at him through eyes of understanding. "What is it your father has commanded you to do?"

Sven looked at her with surprise. "Why do you assume it is father that has asked me to do something?" He became suspicious, and glanced around.

She drew his attention back. "Because I know the man and what he is capable of." Her voice became gentler. "Honey, I spent many years with Ahmed and watched him change from a kind, loving husband to a violent, vindictive man. He came to hate the sight of me and I knew when it happened. From the time he started attending that mosque, his ways changed. I became convinced they were corrupting his mind and he no longer seemed to love anything or anybody."

"You're right about that; he didn't even love me!" he spewed. "I wonder why he didn't let me go with you because he seemed to hate the sight of me and cut me down every chance he got." He shook his head, "I've spent my whole life trying to win his approval."

"Ahmed needed to control someone," she answered quietly; then asked, "Does he control you, Sven?"

Everything suddenly went still as the truth of her words crept into his mind.

27.
Coordination and Connections

Katarina tried to set a time for her to meet her son the following day. Sven hedged about meeting in a restaurant. Bruce knew why; Katarina guessed. She offered, "Since you live in Brooklyn, could we meet in another area of the city for lunch? It doesn't have to be a popular place; maybe something small and out of the way."

Sven thought about it. He didn't want his father to know his mother was in town. He thought about a small Polish restaurant close to their old neighborhood that would be safe. Everyone they knew had moved away so he felt okay about suggesting the place. The restaurant was situated in the basement of an old house and they served delicious food. Oddly enough, most of the clientele were businessmen. He told her where and when, and the two parted.

Bruce complained, "We didn't learn much, but maybe tomorrow she'll be successful in drawing him out. I keep feeling like we don't have much time." Jim felt the same way. They decided to prime Katarina for her meeting.

"Try to get Sven to identify some of his friends. Do it in such a way that he will not become suspicious." Jim then gave her some ideas.

The next order of business was to arrange for two FBI undercover agents to be seated at the adjacent table to the Abadi's.

Ali Madur called Houseman and told him he had made arrangements to pick up the product. He was careful what he said over the phone, remembering how his boss had cautioned him in the event someone was listening. "Would you rather we meet in person so I can give you the details?"

"Yes, yes. I'll meet you at the usual place at seven tonight."

Lockman opened the door and the frigid air rushed in. "The weather sure has turned cold again!" he lamented with a shiver.

"And if all goes according to plan, it'll soon be hot at Grand Central," the older man quipped.

Lockman smirked, "You got that right, boss."

The two made their way into the office. It had the barest of necessities but offered an old leather sofa for guests. "It's been a long day and I'm anxious to hear what Madur has to say," Houseman said, as he took the seat behind the desk.

It wasn't long before there was a knock at the warehouse door. Madur was led to the office and greeted Houseman.

"Tell me what you've been able to locate," demanded the boss.

Madur flopped down onto the sofa, leaning forward. "I was able to secure enough dynamite to replace most of what we need."

Houseman was pleased. "How long do we have before they'll realize some of it's missing?"

"My source says we have about two and a half weeks. According to the forecast, it may rain a couple days next week, which means the job will be put on hold. The stupid Americans use any excuse to get out of work. But it would work to our advantage because it would give us more time before they realize anything is missing."

"Good, good," said Houseman. "How are you going to get it?"

"I figured it wouldn't do to have someone just take it out of the storage room. Eventually, the Feds would start poking around and question the employees. I didn't want anyone connected to me, so I suggested my friend stage a real live robbery; broken locks and all. It would not be realized until they needed the dynamite, which would be much later.

"My friend is bringing it to me day after tomorrow at an agreed location. We'll make sure no street cameras are working there."

"You're thinking, Madur, and I like that," complimented the boss as he added, "I certainly hope you took precautions about not revealing my name to *any*one!"

"Of course," responded Madur.

The three men discussed other relative matters and made arrangements when they would meet again.

When Fred Houseman got home, he went into his study and gave his butler instructions that he was not to be disturbed. He entered his small private space for he was preparing to FaceTime with Pierre in Paris.

"Hello, my friend," greeted the Frenchman.

Houseman was never a friendly sort and most generally cut to the chase. He did so now. "I was successful in obtaining enough dynamite to accomplish our objective; but not as much as I would like. So I would say that March 13th will still be the date."

"So glad to hear it. Have you figured out where the diamonds are?" questioned Pierre.

"No. It still remains a mystery, but their disappearance has certainly caused us to be doubly careful. We have taken additional steps to insure there are no slip-ups."

Houseman told the Frenchman the order in which things were going to happen:

"First of all, we have two fine patriots working at a restaurant at Grand Central. I have several men who will place bombs throughout the structure, from lower levels to the main hall. One of the men who is employed at the restaurant will plant one of the bombs in their kitchen. All of them will be radio activated and will go off according to plan."

"What is the plan?" asked Pierre.

"First, the bomb placed on the lowest level will be detonated. Then the others will go off precisely three minutes after the first one. We intended to have more on the main floor, but we don't have enough explosives to level the entire building. It'll still make a statement, though. Too bad we couldn't get more explosives. I'm sure you realize the reason why the plan was changed."

"Of course, the diamonds. What time will the show begin?"

"At the peak hour for passengers to be in the building, 5:30 pm."

"You are a very clever and wise man, Fred."

The older man allowed himself a smile. "We are ready for our *Friday the thirteenth* surprise. The Americans will forever remember this day just like 9/11. Everything is set, so I presume I won't be talking with you until all is said and done."

Houseman remained seated. *One more dreaded phone call to make,* thought the man. He dialed the number.

"This is Houseman; who am I speaking to?" When he was satisfied the right man was on the other end, he continued. "I'm sure you're wondering why you haven't heard from me and this is the reason why. . ." He explained the disappearance of the diamonds which were to be payment for the dynamite. The man was agitated.

"What would you have me do?" Houseman asked, exasperated. "Look, we had an agreement at which time the explosives would leave your hands and the diamonds would leave mine. There *was* no exchange, therefore I see no reason for you to be unreasonable. You know I will use you in the future, when I have the means to pay you."

The conversation ended with the provider being a little put out, and the would-be purchaser relieved.

As they had planned earlier, Jim and Bruce drove out to see Andy that evening. He was asleep, but glad they woke him. His first question after he opened his eyes was to inquire about Rebecca. "How is she? I think of her continuously."

"She's staying with us until her apartment is put back in order. She'll probably go home in a day or two."

He said with aggravation, "I mean about her pregnancy! How does she feel?"

"Doing good as far as I can tell. She and Beth have become good friends and they shop a lot! What can I say?" Jim answered with a chuckle.

The two men were pleased to see how Andy had improved. He informed them, "Other than a few bruises which change colors daily, my broken fingers and arm are healing nicely, so the doc says. He's relieved I don't have a concussion but he's not sure about my hip; it seems it was damaged and I may need surgery in the future. I sure won't be out dancing anytime soon," he chuckled. "And I might add, without the excellent training I received in service I'd be dead now."

Andy always surprised Jim with his positive outlook on life. He always seemed ready to look at the bright side of things. When Jim had been kidnapped in Atlanta, he had rushed to the captain's rescue with the rest of his old unit. They were still a tight-knit group and Jim recalls at the last reunion they spent most of the time rehashing the rescue. Dave told how he was undercover in a bar and how Andy had protected him; he acted like he'd never seen him before. Now, here he was making light of his own situation!

Bruce announced, "We seem to be making some progress on our case. I should have some news the next time we come out."

"When will that be?" asked the patient.

"Probably a week from now."

The two visitors didn't stay long as they could see Andy was tiring.

28.
The Meeting

The next morning around 11:30, one of the agents arrived at the restaurant ahead of Katarina. He asked the hostess if he could be seated near an empty table as he expected some of his associates to join him. He asked her if she could save it for him for a limited time. It was against policy, but the girl reluctantly agreed because he was so nice; and he also gave her a nice tip which made it easier to bend the rules.

At 11:45, Katarina arrived and the other FBI agent followed her in. She had no idea he was an agent. After the hostess greeted Katarina, the agent interrupted and told the hostess the rest of his party would not be coming and he would be joining his friend already seated. As a result, the table was freed up near them. As the girl led him to his table, he dropped his keys near the adjacent table and when he bent down to retrieve them, quickly planted a listening device under the table top.

The hostess then took Katarina to the table that had just become available. Katarina couldn't keep her eyes off the door; praying Sven would show up. With relief, she saw her handsome son enter. She waved him over and gave him her most winning smile. He returned the smile and it warmed her heart.

"I'm a little late, I had trouble finding a parking space," he apologized as he sat down. He looked around as the place began to fill up. "Man, this restaurant sure has gotten popular since I was here last."

"Did you bring a girlfriend here?"

He looked down at his menu and said, "No. I don't have time to date; I work evenings."

"Where do you work?" she asked with interest.

"At a steak house at Grand Central Station."

"Have you been there long?"

"For about a year now. A friend from the mosque works there as a busboy and he got me an interview. They hired me on the spot." He continued proudly, "And I got promoted to waiter after only six weeks!"

Katarina praised him and asked, "Has your friend, . . .uh, what was his name? Was he promoted also?"

He shook his head, "His name is Gofar. Too bad, but he just doesn't want it bad enough. He's slow and doesn't do a good job."

"I bet you're very quick and thorough."

He grinned, "And how would you know that?"

"Because when you were a little tyke I had to train you to pick up your toys before your father got home. We had such a small apartment that the slightest mess made the whole place look trashed. You knew what to do after the first time I showed you and you were quick about it. We used to make a game of it. I'd say, 'Let's pretend the President is coming for a visit and he'll be here in fifteen minutes!' Together, we immediately started picking up and everything was neat when your father came home.

"Sven was looking off into the distance. "I vaguely remember that, now that you mention it, and father is still a stickler for neatness," said Sven. "Do you remember reading a book to me every night before I went to sleep. . .and sing a song?"

"Sure I do. I looked forward to it every day. And do you remember me kissing you on your nose when I tucked you in?"

"No! Did you do that?" he asked hopefully.

Katarina loved the direction of their conversation but decided she'd better turn the conversation toward getting the info for the FBI. Right after the waitress took their order, she asked, "Did you do well in school, Sven?"

"Not bad, but not great either. I didn't do much homework and I think that affected my grades."

Katarina quietly interjected that it would've been different if she'd been there.

Sven grinned and continued, "In middle school, I made the wrestling team. I did pretty good in the sport and enjoyed it. I continued in high school and became sort of a jock. I had girls trying to get my eye all the time." He thought, *She'll never know the difference if I lie; might as well try to make her proud.*

"Did you ever have a special girl?"

He looked down at his plate, "Yes, there was one girl named Angela and we started becoming serious. When I spoke to her about Islam, she backed off. Both of our fathers were unhappy about our dating and were happy when we broke up. Father told me to choose a Muslim girl and then there wouldn't be a problem with her father *or* him. And then he'd go on one of his tirades about you."

Katarina was shocked. "You mean he even mentioned me that long after I left?"

"Oh yes. I think he had a love/hate relationship with you. One minute he'd be yelling about your abandonment and the next day he might compliment you on being a good homemaker and mother. I couldn't figure him out."

"Sven, do you mind if I ask you about your faith?" She was weak in the knees and glad she wasn't standing.

"Not at all. To save you some time, though, I know you're a Christian and told me stories from the Bible. Father was furious when you did that. He also said he hated you didn't want to convert to Islam."

"How did you become interested in Islam?"

"Father took me to the mosque with him all the time. It was the only time I witnessed a calmness in him. I was curious about something which could bring about a change like that in such an angry man."

"How old were you when you made it your religion?" she asked.

"When I was around twenty-one. Since then I've made some friends at the mosque and we have a good time. I don't know whether you know this or not, but good Muslims don't drink or do drugs. It seems to make most mothers very happy," he said with a sly grin.

"Well, I *am* happy you don't do those things," she said with a giggle. "However, all I remember when your father started going to the mosque was his change in personality. He *hated* so easily and soon it was me he hated above all else. I've never been able to figure it out until recently."

"What did you learn?"

"That when he looked at my blond hair and blue eyes, he realized he made a dreadful mistake marrying out of his faith. And then when he looked at you, there were those baby-blues looking back at him. You had lighter hair when you were a toddler, but it started to turn dark just before I left." Katarina looked into the distance. "You know, Sven, I already told you he put me out of our apartment with a small suitcase, but there wasn't one picture of you! I longed to see you and would imagine what you were doing and how you looked." She looked at him askance. "You've turned into a handsome man, honey."

He blushed. No one ever complimented him or called him 'honey' and he didn't know what to say. So he said nothing. The food was brought to the table, and the two continued their conversation over lunch.

Katarina went on, "I see a glimpse of who you are, son, and I don't see the anger and hate I witnessed in your father. What do you think the reason is?

"I'm not perfect, you're just seeing part of who I am." he muttered.

"Are you saying you have a temper like your father?"

"I'm saying that there are things about me you would not approve of."

"What things, Sven?" she asked softly.

The young man shook his head as if to clear it. His mood seemed to change and he spoke firmly, "I don't want to tell you *what things* and I'm done talking about it!" He sat up straighter.

Katarina saw a glimpse of Sven's father and knew what was happening. There was a war for Sven's soul going on and he had made up his mind to continue the way he was going. Her heart ached for him and she was frantic to change his mind but something inside her seemed to say, "Just love him. He needs love more than anything." She changed the subject immediately.

"I guess you wonder where I've been all these years." Sven nodded. "I'm living on my parent's farm and loving the freedom, the fresh outdoors *and* the work."

Sven asked with surprise, "Do you mean you work on the farm?"

"Yes I do, I'm not a wimp, you know. Sadly, my mother died of cancer several years ago and I'm just thankful I was there to help my dad get through a rough time; he loved her deeply. I was young and able bodied and it happened naturally that I started helping him on the farm."

"Did you ever remarry?" he asked with curiosity.

"No, I didn't. I've never met anyone I was interested in, let alone love. It's as if I've been burned too bad."

Sven dropped his eyes. He knew he could love his mother again, but too much had happened recently. It just wasn't in the cards. At least he was trying to convince himself of that. He looked up, "Can you tell me about your childhood?"

For some time, Katarina regaled him with story after story of a young girl growing up on a large farm in Wisconsin. She told him of her dreams of going to the big city and getting a job; of meeting someone and falling in love. After high school, she went to secretarial school for one year. She saved her money and against her parent's wishes, went to New York. Shortly after her arrival, she got a job in a real estate office and was lucky to find a roommate to share expenses. One weekend, she and her roommate went to the park and that's where she met Ahmed.

Sven wanted to know more, but Katarina was too saddened to go on. Sharing all of her hopes and dreams and how they were dashed was more than she could handle right now. She became quiet.

"When are you returning to Wisconsin?" asked her son.

"The end of next week and I was hoping I could convince you to come with me." She added, "for a visit, of course."

Sven's mind started racing and he thought, *what a perfect solution! I'll return to Wisconsin with my mother after the bombing and I'll be out of the state when all hell breaks loose.* "You know, that sounds great. I've saved some money and I can afford to fly with you! What day are you returning?" he asked.

"On Friday, March 13th." Katarina saw Sven's excitement dry up. "What is it, Sven?"

"I have some important plans I can't cancel for Friday evening." He looked hopeful, "Do you think you could postpone your return until Saturday afternoon?"

Katarina looked at the young man and replied, "I'll certainly try. Shall I make a reservation for two for Saturday afternoon?"

He grinned with enthusiasm, "Yes, absolutely."

"What about your job?" she asked.

"I'm due for vacation time and they like me. I won't have any trouble."

She laughed at his delight and said, "It would please me if you called me 'mom' or 'mother'."

He gave her an endearing smile and said, "Okay, Mom."

Katarina called for a cab and the two hugged goodbye on the sidewalk. She whispered in his ear, "I'm going to continue to pray for you non-stop." The cab approached, and she was gone. Sven walked in the opposite direction to his truck.

When Katarina got in the cab, she gave him the address of FBI headquarters. The cab driver glanced at her in his rearview mirror. That was Sven Abadi hugging the beautiful blond woman in the back seat. Sven had her eyes; she *must* be the mother who had abandoned her husband and child. The cabbie was best friends with Ahmed and he would want to know this. He needed to take the fare to her address as quickly as possible and then talk with Ahmed; most importantly telling him of where he dropped her off.

29.
What to Do, What to do?

Ahmed Abadi arrived home at the usual time. His son blew past him on his way to work with barely a "bye."

"Wait," called his father. "Have you been to prayer today?"

"No time. I'll talk with you when I get home tonight." The young man hoofed it out the door and Ahmed heard him peal off toward the subway.

The man was taking some food out of the refrigerator when he heard the doorbell ring. "He clicked on the speaker and inquired, "Who is it?"

"Your best friend, Jamaal."

Ahmed pressed the buzzer for the front door. Shortly there came a knock at the door. He smiled with a greeting when he opened the door, but received a sour scowl in return. "What's eating you?" Ahmed inquired.

"You'll never guess what happened to me today." He planned to draw the conversation out; this *was* the best bit of news he'd ever had.

"Have you eaten supper, yet?" asked Ahmed.

"Forget food. What I have to tell you can trump food!"

Ahmed sighed. He was used to Jamaal's theatrics, and he said with resignation, "Go ahead. Tell me."

Jamaal started with the call to pick up a woman at a restaurant in their old neighborhood. When he got there, a man was hugging a woman on the street." He paused for effect. "It was Sven. When the woman got in my cab, she gave me an address and I checked her out in my rearview mirror. She had blue eyes like Sven's; and the blondest hair. . .the kind not out of a bottle. You couldn't miss the resemblance. I think she was Sven's mother!" He waited for the fireworks.

Ahmed remained motionless. He turned toward Jamaal, with a bowl in his hand. Without any notice, he threw the bowl against the wall, breaking it into small shards with food dripping down the wall.

He was furious and his face showed it.

Jamaal continued, "And you'll never guess where she had me take her. . .to FBI headquarters!"

Ahmed fell into a chair at the table. His eyes were dark and menacing. "Where did Sven go?" he shouted.

"I don't know. He headed in the opposite direction from my cab. Do you think he'll tell you he met her today?"

"I'm not sure. He believes in what we're planning to do and considers it an honor to be chosen to take such an important part. But you never know if that *she-devil* has entered the picture. As a little kid, Sven loved her very much. He was crushed when she left and watched for her to walk through our apartment door every single night for months. I thought I'd never get him to accept the fact she was gone forever."

"What 'important part' does Sven have?" asked Jamaal.

"You know better than to ask that question. Just know that it's very important!" The irate father was turning ideas over in his mind. To himself he thought, *It isn't a coincidence she tried to connect with Sven now. Since Jamaal took her to the FBI, we can assume they suspect something's up. How in the world did Sven appear on their radar?*

He spoke to his friend, "I need to think this through carefully. Give me some time and I would ask you to not to share this information with anyone until after I call you. Can you do that for an old friend, Jamaal?"

The man agreed and left.

The temptation to tell Lockman this juicy bit of news was about all Jamaal could do to keep it to himself. He knew he would score points with Lockman if he told him now, and it might give Jamaal a chance to become one of the inner circle. After careful consideration, he decided to give Ahmed the time he asked for.

Ahmed made sure he was in bed when Sven came in. He wasn't ready to confront him and hadn't figured out how he was going to do it. He remained in bed until he was sure Sven was sound asleep. One thing he knew about his son, Sven hit the bed and went to sleep instantly.

Around 1:30 am, the father got up and slipped into Sven's room. He picked up his son's jeans and tiptoed out of the room. After locking the bathroom door, he went through his pockets. He found Sven's cell and began checking his calls. There it was! An out-of-state number. He would bet money it was a call from

Katarina. He memorized the number.

Bruce Foster and the other agents on the case, listened to the conversation between Sven Abadi and his mother at the restaurant. When Katarina had balked about wearing a wire again, he agreed but didn't tell her the conversation would be recorded anyway. He listened with interest.

After they heard the entire discourse, Bruce sat in his chair contemplating the few bits of information they now had. Friday night was important; it had to be the night they were planning an attack. Sven was reluctant to share 'what things' with his mother; in fact, it put him on the defensive. He also said there were things about him that Katarina would disapprove of. *She sure would disapprove if she found out that Sven was part of a terrorist group that planned an attack on the U.S.!*

That evening, Foster made himself available to take Katarina back to her hotel and out to dinner again. This time they did talk about Katarina's lunch with Sven. She seemed to be more comfortable with Bruce every time he saw her.

After a sleepless night, Ahmed had made a plan to thwart any plan Katarina *or* the FBI might have. He went into the kitchen and made a pot of coffee; then he went into Sven's room and shook him awake. "Wake up! I have something important I need to talk to you about."

Sven threw his legs out of bed, looked at the clock, and grumbled about having to get up so early. He stumbled into the bathroom, threw some cold water on his face, and went into the kitchen. His father was sitting at the table sipping a cup of coffee. He poured himself a cup and sat down across from his father.

Without preamble, Ahmed spoke. "My friend, Jamaal, has been driving a cab in New York City for many years now. He took a call yesterday from a woman at a restaurant. When he pulled up, the woman was hugging a man on the sidewalk. It was *you*, Sven. When the lady got in the cab, you headed off in the opposite direction. The woman gave Jamaal the address where she wanted to go. He looked at her in the rearview mirror and saw a blond with blue eyes and said you looked just like her." He paused to allow the importance of the information to sink in. "She told Jamaal to take her to FBI headquarters!"

Sven looked like he had been sucker-punched. He didn't know what to say or do. He looked down into his coffee, wondering why his mother wanted to go to the FBI.

"Were you going to tell me your mother had made contact with you? And how long have you been sneaking around with her?" His fist hit the table. "LOOK AT ME!"

He looked up, his eyes wide. "Two days ago, she showed up after work. We went for a ride and she told me the truth why she left." He looked at his father with loathing. "You've been lying to me all these years. You're a sick s.o.b."

Ahmed lunged across the table and smacked his son across the face. The coffee went flying. "You think you know so much, don't you. Well I'll tell you, your mother is nothing but a dirty infidel. She had a chance to embrace the faith but refused and I knew right then she wasn't capable of raising a good Muslim boy with the right values. I tried to *save* you from her and her warped religion." He was sweating and his face was red as a beet. Sven thought he might have a heart attack or stroke.

The young man stood up and paced the small kitchen. "I listened to what she had to say and figured it had to be the truth. I remember how you used to treat her and it scared both of us."

"And did she listen to what *you* had to say?" He grinned sadistically. "And what did you tell *her*?"

"Nothing of importance; I can tell you that. She asked some benign questions, like did I have a girlfriend and did I have a job. She asked if I had a temper like you. I just told her in so many words that I wasn't perfect. She didn't press me."

"Why do you think she went to FBI headquarters?" asked his father.

"I have no idea. There wasn't one thing I told her that would give her any idea that a terrorist attack is coming!" Sven had an awful feeling in his gut when he remembered telling her that he was busy with something very important next Friday night. He decided to keep that part of the conversation to himself. "We then planned to have lunch the next day as she's returning home soon." Sven felt good about his sins of omission; *after all, what father doesn't know won't hurt him.*

Ahmed told Sven to sit down. He looked into the face of his son and when he looked into those blue eyes, he felt like he was looking at Katarina. It made him mad all over again. How stupid to be taken in by appearance; he should have looked for a dark-haired Muslim girl with brown eyes and then they wouldn't be in this mess.

"We have to find out if Katarina is in cahoots with the FBI. Do you think you can find that out?" Ahmed asked with derision.

"I guess I could call her and meet her somewhere. I don't even know where she's staying!"

"Good, good. First of all, make sure she's alone. Then you start talking and *you* control the conversation. Begin by asking her if she knows anyone in New York anymore. Ask her where she's staying. Ask her why the cabbie, your father's best friend, took her to FBI headquarters. Then watch her squirm." His sadistic grin made Sven sick.

The young man was having mixed emotions. Sven didn't want to trap her into admitting to something he didn't want to hear. Then again, he was mad to think she may be using him. He felt like asking, w*ill the real Katarina Abadi please stand up!* He knew something had to be done right away. Lockman would be livid if he were privy to this information and then what would happen to their plans? What would happen to *him?* Sven realized he had some serious soul-searching to do and said to his father, "I need to go to the mosque to pray."

His father was surprised, to put it mildly. He was supposed to be the good Muslim but he didn't even consider going to the mosque when the problem confronted him.

30.
Coffee

Ahmed called his cabbie friend and told him what had happened with Sven that morning. He asked, "Did you tell anyone about what you saw yesterday?"

The man replied, "You asked me to keep it to myself until I heard from you. I honored your request."

"I'm glad, Jamaal; you're a good friend. I have a plan, but it will take a couple of days."

The following day, the agents were having a cup of coffee in the break room when Katarina's cell rang; it was Sven. He asked her where she was staying and then suggested a small coffee shop close by where they could talk. They were to meet at 4:00 before he went to work. Katarina told Bruce what had just transpired. He thought for a moment and said, "Katarina, be careful!"

"I'll be careful." She looked at him and searched his eyes. "Do you think he would hurt me?" she asked.

"None of us know. This is uncharted territory and you've been out of his life for many years. You don't really know, after two short meetings, what kind of a man Sven is or where his loyalties lie. As you said yourself, Ahmed is a brutal man with enough anger for a regiment. He's the one who raised your son."

She thought about what he said and agreed with him. "I want so badly to think the best of him. I keep thinking about the little boy I birthed and hopefully the impact I had on him for five years. I taught him how to respect others, about being honest, about showing loving kindness, and about love. I have to believe the impact I made didn't disappear entirely after I left."

Bruce kept still, saying nothing.

"As you know I don't want to wear a wire, but I understand how you feel about it; you need to keep track of what is going on." She looked at him with a coquettish grin. "I was surprised you had a listening device planted under the table at lunch. I must say I was a little perturbed with you."

"Better for you to be perturbed than in trouble," he refuted.

"I will wear a wire this time if you insist."

When the two returned from break, her wire was put in place. Afterward, she went into the conference room and saw a person talking with Bruce. He turned and introduced the agent. "This is Jenny Remington and she'll be as close to you as she can get without Sven being aware. Do you have any questions?"

"None that I can think of."

Katarina entered the coffee shop about five minutes early. She saw an elderly woman seated on a stool at the counter. When the woman turned to look at her, then turned around, she thought, S*urely that can't be Jenny!* It *was* Jenny Remington in a perfect disguise. She completely ignored Katarina's presence. What Katarina didn't know was the mirror behind the counter gave Jenny a birds eye view of Katarina's table.

Soon Sven came in. He glanced around, making note there was only one old woman at the counter. He sat down next to Katarina, saying, "Hi, Mom."

"Hi. I'm so glad you called! I'll take any extra time I can get with you," she said lightheartedly, patting his arm.

"I feel the same way. You know, after we left the restaurant, I kept thinking of things that I wanted to ask you. Do you mind if we catch up some more?"

"Not at all, Sven. Fire away."

He felt lousy asking her, but he jumped right in. "Do you still know people in New York? I would have thought you lost touch with everyone after so many years."

"I don't know anyone but you and your father. I came to New York to locate you; I wanted to tell you the truth about why I left. I felt like you were old enough to make up your own mind about me. After all, it was only fair for you to hear my side of the story, too."

Sven was relieved. He asked her if she liked her hotel.

Katarina told him it was fine and explained she'd made reservations for a full week. She said she didn't know how long it would take to find him.

He seemed satisfied; now the hard part: "The cabbie that picked you up in front of the restaurant happens to be father's best friend. He couldn't wait to tell him about the beautiful blond with the blue-blue eyes he saw hugging me on the sidewalk. When he looked at you in the rearview mirror, he saw the resemblance between us. Then he told father he took you to FBI headquarters!"

Katarina just sat there, shocked. What bad luck that Ahmed's friend would witness their embrace AND tell him where she went. She was at a loss as to what to say.

"Mom, why did you go to FBI headquarters?"

Bruce and Jim were sitting in a car down the street from the coffee shop when they heard the part about the cabbie. They jumped out of their car and quickly made their way to the shop. This wasn't at all what they expected!

31.
Scrambling

Jim Redmon walked into the coffee shop and approached the counter. He ordered a coffee and took it over to Katarina's table. Sven looked up sharply, questioning.

"Hello, Katarina. And this must be your son, Sven."

Sven looked at his mother and spoke with a hiss, "Who is *he?*" He eased his chair back a little, as if he were ready to take off.

"He's a new friend of mine, Sven. And he isn't with the FBI!"

The young man looked at his mother, then asked Jim, "Why are you here?"

Jim talked softly so he wouldn't spook him. "I'm here to help your mother, Sven. I'm sure you can understand how worried she is about you. Can we talk frankly?"

"What do you want to talk about?"

Jim knew that his next words were critical. "About the organization you belong to and the disastrous plans you have planned."

Sven was shocked that so much was known about him. He wondered if they knew exactly what was planned and his part in it. He glared at his mother; *she is part of this and tricked me into believing she wanted a relationship with me.* With disappointment, he turned to his mother, "So all of what you said to me was a lie to get me to give you information?"

Katarina shook her head vehemently. "Not so, Sven. Most of it was the truth because I did want a chance to tell you why I really left you."

Jim interjected, "What your mother said is true. I'm a private detective and I was here in New York looking into the death of my good friend. The evidence led to Fred Houseman and his men. From there, the FBI realized I was getting close to the truth and asked me to join forces with them. They found out a terrorist attack was in the works. Just suffice it to say the clues directed us to you and they approached your mother to see if she'd be willing to help.

This information should be enough to convince you the FBI is aware of a planned attack."

This was staggering information to Sven. He looked like a caged animal looking for a way to escape. Just then, Bruce Foster walked in. He approached the table and said, "I think we can talk more privately back at our headquarters, Sven. You can leave peaceably or I can cuff you; it's up to you."

You could tell the young man was weighing his options and escaping from this situation wasn't realistic. He said softly, "I'll walk out peaceably." The group left the shop and drove to FBI Headquarters where they exited at a private entrance.

In the car, Sven refused to look at his mother. He was perspiring, in spite of the cold weather. They were sitting in the back of the sedan and Katarina reached over, putting her hand over his. He started to jerk away, but she grasped his hand. With the traffic noise, she felt she could speak privately to her son. Quietly, she whispered, "Sven, do you believe what I said about why I left our home and you?"

He still kept his eyes riveted on the front windshield, but he nodded.

"Do you believe that I love you now and never stopped loving you?"

Sven was very still. She could tell he was thinking and didn't dare ruin the moment by continuing.

After a few minutes, the concerned mother spoke, "I want you to know I am a Christian and my religion is based on love. I tried to teach you that when you were a little boy, but I had only five short years with you. Your father's form of Islam is based on hate; and it drove a wedge between us. I believe with all my heart that Ahmed loved me very much when we got married. When I was around seven months pregnant, he started attending the mosque. I thought he wanted to be prepared to be a good father. But the man in charge of the mosque was filled with hate. The first time I witnessed this was when I named you after my father. Ahmed never did get over it."

Katarina allowed what she said to settle in Sven's mind. She said nothing for about five minutes.

Finally, Sven turned to her and said, "I only have a few short memories of our time together; but one thing I always knew was that you loved me. I just couldn't understand why you left me with father."

Tears glazed over Katarina's eyes. She looked at her son and said, "And now you know that I would never have left if he hadn't threatened our lives. Dear God, I don't want you to do anything you will regret for the rest of your life. I'm not sure what plans your organization has for you, but I pray it will not have anything to do with taking a human life. I can't fathom you being a terrorist! It breaks my heart to even consider it."

The young man looked out the side window. There were a million thoughts going through his mind. *After all, what is an infidel; not this gentle woman sitting beside him who spoke of her faith with such love. As far as he could tell, she believed as strongly about her religion as his father did about his. Only one big difference: she spoke in love and father spoke with reviling hatred.* Sven realized he was sitting on the fence about what he truly believed.

When the group entered the conference room, all eyes were on Sven. Bruce Foster felt sorry for him and wanted to soft-peddle the interrogation for Katarina's sake. There was too much riding on this though, and a whole lot of innocent lives were at stake. Being a stalwart professional, he conducted himself the way the FBI trained him.

"Sven, we've been hearing from our sources that something big is expected to go down soon. As Jim Redmon explained to you, your mother was located and asked to come here and try to find out if you were implicated. Along with other information, we now know that you are implicated.

"Have you even considered what will happen if this terrorist attack is successful? There will be men, women and possibly children killed or maimed. And for what? To convince Americans that you sincerely believe Christianity and the United States of America are works of the devil and that Islam is a far superior way?" He let the words sink in and shook his head, "It's hard for me to believe that this false sort of thinking can be embraced by so many people!"

Foster began his serious questioning: "Tell me how Lockman is involved? We know he hosts a meeting at his house and you've been seen going in and out." Sven could hardly believe it. *They DO know something big is planned!* He looked over at his mother. Her face was pleading with him; he felt like he could almost read her mind. She nodded at him, urging him to tell them what he knew.

The young man gathered up his courage and said, "Lockman is the supervisor of Houseman's warehouse. He is the only one we see; Mr. Houseman has never met with us but we know he is the brains of the outfit."

"How did you become involved, Sven?"

"Through the dogged determination of my father. He wanted more than anything for me to become completely accepted by these men. He would tell them every chance he got how dedicated I was to the faith and their vision. . .and he'd add how smart I was. I think father was trying to live his dreams through me. When they asked me if I wanted to serve Allah in this, I could almost see my father salivate. HE would have liked to be the one who was chosen. Lockman talked with me several times and my father prepared me for his questions. He was satisfied, and mentioned how perfect it was I already had a job at Grand Central, and I didn't *look* like a middle easterner."

Jim thought, *The terminal HAS to be the site they're going to hit!* He knew Bruce had the same thought, by the look on his face.

The agents asked Sven several more questions about his job. He told them his friend from the mosque had gotten him a job as a busboy as he already worked there. He seemed pleased to relate how impressed management was with his work ethic and how they promoted him to a waiter soon after he started. "Gohar is *still* a busboy!" he boasted.

Bruce continued, "We feel pretty sure that the attack will occur next Friday night. Are we right in our assumption, Sven?"

The young man nodded, continually surprised at how much the FBI knew.

Jim interjected, "Have you been given any instructions about what you are to do and when?" Bruce was surprised Jim had spoken, but his question was right on track.

"No. We're to get our final instructions next Thursday night at Lockman's house. We've been ordered to come at seven."

Bruce asked, "I'm curious. How do they plan for you to get out before the blast? Or are you to be a suicide bomber?"

Sven was startled. "NO WAY," he said with alarm. "This isn't a suicide mission. I do know there are those chosen who will place the explosives on Friday. I'm not sure where, but there'll be some on the lower level, on the main concourse, at the front door, and I'm to place the one in our restaurant. I'm not sure how they'll be detonated. I guess we'll learn that on Thursday night."

Another agent asked, "Are the men who are placing the bombs part of the group that meets at Lockman's house?"

"I think so. The reason I say that is Lockman has given us strict instructions not to talk to anyone about this. He said there's a small core-group of people who know about it and he said he'd kill the first one to open their trap!" Sven paused, "And I believe him."

Katarina and every agent in the room realized Sven had finally made a life or death decision to work with the FBI by providing them this information. For him, there was no turning back. Katarina was very proud but also frightened for her son's safety.

The agents asked several more questions as to whether Sven had any idea where the explosives were coming from. He told them he didn't have a clue.

One agent cautioned Sven to be very careful about what he said. He indicated that one little sentence could place him in jeopardy. He also encouraged him to act as if nothing had happened. He said, "I know your father can probably read you pretty well. Most fathers can," he said with a knowing grin, "so he'll pick up on any play-acting you may do. Try to be natural with him, without telling him anything."

Bruce declared, "Sven, we're going to have to come up with a plan to get the information you receive on Thursday night. We'll work something out and perhaps arrange for you to send us word through your mother. We're going to think about it and we'll get back to you. I want you to know that we're going to continue to keep this operation very quiet for your safety. You have my word on it."

"I'm sure glad of that!" Sven murmured with sarcasm. He looked at his mother and the pride was so evident on her face that he took pleasure in it. She motioned that she'd call him.

Bruce and Jim walked over to Sven and shook his hand. It was a signal the meeting was over and one by one everyone left the room.

Jim called Manny to come pick him up. They would drive Sven to his truck and let him continue on to work. It wouldn't do to call a cab; the cabbie may be someone Sven or his father knew.

32.
Clandestine Activities

When Ahmed arrived home that evening, he saw a note from Sven. It read, "Meeting mother at four. She's staying at the Nobel Hotel."

The man was pleased for it meant that what he had said to Sven had gotten through to him. He was *not* pleased that he was meeting Katarina again so soon. He picked up his cell and called Jamaal, asking him to come by when he was free.

When the cabbie arrived, the two sat down in the living room. Ahmed started pacing and talking to Jamaal like he was giving a speech to the faithful at the mosque. Jamaal looked at him quizzically, thinking his friend might be losing it.

"Do you agree that this situation must be resolved? This is a good Muslim man I'm trying to protect," stated the zealous father.

"Yes. I agree with you, Ahmed. But what can you possibly do? Sven has done nothing wrong; it's his mother who has brought this on. If what you say is true, he didn't give any important information to her. I say wait it out; she'll be gone soon."

"Don't you realize she'll be here at the most crucial time for us? Just knowing that she's talking with the feds at this time isn't a coincidence. I can't have her trying to trick Sven into divulging any information. And I don't know how cunning she has been so far; he *wants* to believe she still loves him." Ahmed was becoming more worked up and it was apparent to Jamaal. The friend had also learned about when things were going to happen. Here Ahmed was accusing Sven of doing what he had just done! He had practically revealed to Jamaal something was going to happen the coming week.

"I know you haven't asked for my advice, Ahmed, but here it is anyway. I think you should tell Lockman what has happened. He'll take care of it."

"NO, absolutely not! I worked too hard for him to include Sven in this plan and I'll do nothing to change that; I will take care of this.

What I want from you is to run me by the Nobel Hotel so I can scope it out."

"That I can do," replied his friend.

Jim was having a cup of coffee with Beth when his cell rang. It was around seven o'clock in the evening and they had just finished dinner.

Stevens' number appeared on the cell. "Hey Stevens. What's up?"

"That's just what I was going to ask you. I haven't heard from you in awhile and I'm curious what's happening with the case."

Jim was uncomfortable. So *much* had happened, none of which he was at liberty to share with the detective. "Things have sort of come to a stand-still, Bob. I can't seem to get any information from the hospital records department, *or* the ambulance company. Until I get some breaks, I guess things are dead in the water."

"Well if you need anything from me, let me know. By the way, I did find out some interesting facts about Ralph Mercer. His patrolman friend is an Arab; a man without a blemish on his record. In fact, his boss seems to be impressed with him."

"Can you give me his name?"

"Joseph Samad."

"Do you have any other helpful information about him? I'm trying to keep a list of all the people involved in this case."

"He attends that mosque that we're watching. Bunch of dangerous people over there, but we can't touch them. Freedom of religion they call it."

The two ended the conversation with some pleasantries and said their good-byes. Beth looked interested. "You're in a hard place, aren't you honey? You'd like to tell Bob what's happening but you can't."

"You described it succinctly!"

Jamaal and Ahmed made their way into mid-town to the hotel. On their way, Ahmed told him he would go in and check out the lobby. He noticed it was a nice family hotel with a small coffee shop and a bar just off the lobby. He approached the front desk and asked if he could leave a message for Mrs. Abadi. The man told him to write it out and he'd put it in her box. Ahmed waited for the man to put the message in Katarina's box, room 321. Then he asked where he would be able to talk with someone in Housekeeping or Maintenance. He was told to go around to the back of the building and enter the door marked *Deliveries*. Someone there could help him.

Ahmed got back into Jamaal's cab and directed him to the alley around the back. He explained his plan.

When the door opened, a bell rang. A man appeared and asked, "May I help you?"

"Yes. I have an unusual request. My daughter ran away from home about six months ago and I found out she has a job here at the Nobel Hotel in Housekeeping. She was hired under another name. Is there any way I could observe the women working here without being seen? I'm not interested in making a scene so I didn't want to confront her on one of the floors."

The man seemed to be a compassionate sort, for he told Ahmed that the girls didn't come in until around 7:30 am and left at four.

Ahmed whined, "Could I go into their changing room and just get a feel for where she's been?" He acted like a broken-hearted father.

"Sure, I don't think that would be a problem. I'll lead you back there and give you some time."

Ahmed was delighted. He followed the man back and sat down on a bench, lowering his head as if in prayer. The man discretely left the room. The minute he left, Ahmed looked around for key-cards. He saw a cart with a combination of replacement products as well as a master key-card. He pocketed the card, and left the room thanking the man for his kind consideration.

Bruce offered to take Katarina back to her hotel. Two other agents slyly grinned at each other.

"Would you like to go get something to eat before I take you back?" he asked.

"That would be great. I certainly don't have anything to do," she said with a smile.

Bruce drove them to a different restaurant this time, and once again they had a lovely evening. When they were on their way back to the hotel, Bruce asked Katarina if she was going to try to meet with Sven again. She misunderstood and quickly said, "Yes. And I really don't want the FBI nosing into every meeting that I have with my son." She looked out the side window, obviously miffed.

"I didn't mean to rile you, Katarina. It was just a thought and, no, we don't expect to ask you to wear a wire or have someone follow you." He stole a glance her way, "I just don't want anything bad to happen to you."

She seemed to thaw. "I guess I just started thinking of you as a personal friend, rather than a FBI agent. My mistake. I guess I'm starving for friendships."

Bruce took her hand. "I *am* more than an agent. . .to you, at least. After we get to your hotel, let's go into the bar and talk this out."

All she would do was nod.

Abadi decided to go back to the hotel and wait until Katarina returned. He knew it could take all evening, but he wanted to know what she was doing and with whom. He chose a place in the lobby against the wall, partially hidden by a large planter. No one even looked his way. That suited him just fine.

He was just about to call it a night when Katarina entered the lobby with a tall, good-looking man behind her. The man had his hand placed lightly on the small of her back. He was shocked at how beautiful she was. He loved her and he hated her at that moment. The man at the desk called her over and went to her box to retrieve the note Ahmed had left. She opened it, read it, and was confused by its content. She looked up at the man with her and they continued into the bar.

"*Slut!*" he thought. *"Drinking and carrying on with another man. She has no idea how to conduct herself like a good woman. I'm glad I kicked her out of our lives!"* He was seething as he left the hotel.

Katarina and Bruce sat at a table near the window. There were very few customers in the bar, and they had privacy. She showed him the note. It said, "I plan to see you while you are in New York."

Bruce immediately looked around. He went to the bar's entrance and scoped out the lobby but saw no one of interest. He went back to the table, sat down and took Katarina's hands in his. "This puts a new slant on things. I'm *really* concerned for your safety now, Katarina. We need to ask Sven if he told his father where you were staying."

She looked into his eyes, fright in her own. "I agree. Even with the FBI behind me, I'm scared to death of Ahmed. He's very vindictive and wouldn't hesitate to hurt me."

"Not if I can help it," he said. "After we finish our drinks, I insist I go up to your room with you to make sure you have no unwelcome surprises." Her look of relief said it all.

As they approached her room, Bruce took the key-card from her and unlocked the door. He took his gun out and quietly stepped into the room, motioning for her to remain where she was. He checked under the bed, the bathroom and closet and was satisfied the room was empty. Only then did he motion her in.

She stepped in and let out a loud sigh, leaning against the wall. Bruce went to her and gathered her in his arms. She seemed to let all the tension out when his arms went around her. He held her close and she felt safe.

Katarina looked up at him, and he leaned down and kissed her softly. She responded. Bruce knew he had to get out of there as quickly as possible or this was going to get out of hand. They broke their embrace and he said softly, "I need to go, Katarina. Not because I want to, but because I want things to be done right. You know I'm attracted to you, and I think you feel the same way." She nodded those baby-blues at him. He was struck at how vulnerable she was and he refused to take advantage of that. He stepped back, saying, "I'll call you in the morning. Sleep well, my Nordic princess." And he slipped out the door.

Katarina went over and fell on the bed. She hadn't felt this way about a man since she fell in love with Ahmed. Could something so wonderful happen so quickly?

33.
Serenity

The following morning, Bruce called Katarina the minute he got up. He hadn't been able to get to sleep after leaving her. The minute his eyes opened, she was the first one in his thoughts. "Hey sleepyhead. Did you have a good night's sleep?" he asked.

"I had a hard time getting to sleep, but after that I slept like a baby."

"Me too. How long have you been awake?"

"Not long. I'm just lying here thinking about Sven," she paused, "and you."

His heart did a flip-flop. He felt playful, giddy, and thrilled. "I was wondering if you'd made plans yet for today? I thought you'd like to do something fun, or have lunch, or anything with me."

She giggled, "I think it would be fun to do something with you, but I haven't called Sven yet. I'd like to sort of keep my calendar clear for the day until I talk with him. Could I call you?"

"Sure," he replied. "Regardless, I'd like to invite you out to dinner, but this time it would be a date on my dollar instead of the FBI!"

She laughed, "I know Sven works tonight, so that ought to work out great. Should I plan on it?"

"Absolutely. If you find out you have some time after being with Sven, call me and we'll find something to do, even if it's a walk in the park on a cold March day."

"Okay. I'll call you as soon as I know."

Ahmed had a hard time getting to sleep also. In fact, he didn't get much sleep at all. Sven was in the kitchen when he wandered in. He looked at his father and said, "Man, you must have had a hard night!"

"You're right. I have a terrific headache," the man growled.

"Maybe a cup of coffee might help."

As he stepped toward the coffeepot, he looked at his son with renewed interest. "Any plans for today?"

"I thought I'd hang out with Gohar. We thought we'd play some video games at his place."

With a burst of pleasure, Ahmed realized Sven didn't have plans with Katarina. He grunted, "Good, good. You two haven't done anything in awhile."

"Yeah. Every night we work 'til late so sometimes we sleep 'til noon. There isn't much time for fun before we have to go back to work again."

"You two enjoy. I'm going into work soon; a little overtime never hurts."

After Sven got out of the shower, his phone rang. It was his mother.

"Do you have any plans today, Sven? If you didn't, I thought we could spend some time together."

"I *did* make some plans with a friend, but not until after lunch. Gofar likes to sleep in."

"I understand. Why don't you come over to my hotel and I'll treat you to breakfast in the hotel's coffee shop? I understand they're known for their good breakfasts."

"That sounds good."

She grinned, "Great, how long before you can be here?"

"I could be there in thirty minutes. I just got out of the shower."

"I'll meet you in the coffee shop."

Sven was happy his father had already left for work by the time Katarina called. He knew his father was livid that he was seeing her. *Like I've said before, what father doesn't know won't hurt him.*

Even though it was Saturday morning, it was still hard to find a parking place in New York City. When he finally approached the coffee shop, he saw his mother sitting in a booth, waiting for him. She smiled as he walked toward her. She had on a soft powder blue sweater and jeans. *My mother is beautiful!* he thought.

"Good morning, son." Her smile was inviting.

"Hi. I'm glad you called," he said as he sat down. "I was going to settle for a bowl of cereal, but the smells in here have changed my mind." She chuckled. "I know I'm hounding you, but you've got to understand the desire of a mother who hasn't seen her child for years." She looked at him with admiration. "Just *seeing* you is a treat."

The two talked through breakfast, and lingered over coffee. She told her son that she had studied many books on Islam over the years. He was surprised.

"I knew that was how your father was going to raise you and I wanted to know exactly what it was all about."

Sven was all ears. "What stood out to you as you studied?"

She thought for a moment, "I guess it was finding out how important Muhammad is to all Muslims and I didn't realize he was born in 570 A.D. Muslims believe it is Muhammad who has given Islam bodily form."

"I'm impressed that you did all that studying. You probably know more than I know when it comes down to it."

"Perhaps. I wonder how much you know about Christianity? Have you ever read any of the Bible?"

"Father would have killed me if he found a Bible in our house. He told me what I needed to know about being a good Muslim and felt that was all I needed to know."

"Did he insist you attend classes for religious instruction at the mosque?"

"He tried, and I went a couple of times, but I dug in deep and he couldn't persuade me regardless of what he threatened." Sven was pensive.

Katarina continued, "You know, the 9/11 terrorists hurt Islam more than anything. After that happened, many average Muslims wanted to distance themselves from a violent picture of Islam. It's supposed to be a religion of peace, yet there are people like your organization that don't believe that. They want to attack our country because we don't believe the way they do. There are many fine people from many religions residing here in the US and they all feel their way is the right way; yet they co-exist in peace."

Sven was uncomfortable. "I can't believe I've been so gullible and believed everything he said. I never once decided to check it out on my own. It's like I've been brainwashed."

"That's a good way to put it, son."

They were having a wonderful discussion and Katarina hated breaking the mood, but she had to find out if Sven had told his father where she was staying. She thought she'd be up-front about it.

"When I got back to the hotel last night, I had a message in my box. It was a surprise, to say the least. No one knows where I'm staying but you and the FBI." She pulled the note out of her purse and showed it to Sven. His surprise was evident. "Is this Ahmed's handwriting?"

Sven nodded, a look of concern on his face. "I left him a note yesterday saying I was meeting you for coffee and that you were staying at the Nobel Hotel. I never dreamed he'd come here!"

"It frightened me, Sven. I've had too much history with him and I understand how easy it is to set him off. He wouldn't hesitate to hurt me to teach me a lesson."

The concern on her son's face made her realize that he, too, understood the man's volatility. She wondered how many times in his short life that he had suffered the results of Ahmed's anger. It made her feel uneasy.

"Mom, you need to tell Bruce Foster about the note. I don't like it!"

"I've already talked to him. He's very concerned and told me to be careful."

The two commiserated and finished their morning together. Katarina walked him to the hotel entrance and gave him a big hug. "I love you and I'm praying for you non-stop."

Katarina went upstairs and sat in the chair thinking about her time with Sven. She loved that he was concerned for her but she was as concerned for him since he had entered a no-return zone with the FBI. She prayed her son wouldn't be harmed in any way because of it. She had to put it in the Lord's hands; she could do nothing.

After a time, Katarina called Bruce and told him she was free for the rest of the day.

"How did it go with Sven?" He purposely didn't want to ask specific questions for fear Katarina would think he was questioning her as an agent.

"I'll tell you all about it when I see you."

"I'll leave here in the next ten minutes. Wear a warm coat and gloves; we're going to take a walk; it's beautiful, but cold outside." Katarina was to wait in the lobby. He was delighted for he'd have her to himself for the majority of the day and evening. He chuckled to himself, *for some reason I want to be with her all the time.*

The couple went to Central Park and meandered around the cold walkways. There were a few runners out, but not many people just out for a stroll. Bruce took Katarina's hand as they walked. She tingled with excitement and snuggled closer to him

She shared about her time with Sven and his admission that he had told his father about where she was staying. She made sure

Bruce knew it had happened *before* he had come on board with the FBI.

He laughed. "It sure doesn't take long for a mama to go into protection mode for her child! It's okay, Katarina. Sven had no idea what his father would do with the information."

After their walk, they stopped for a cup of hot chocolate. Her cheeks were rosy, her eyes sparkled, and she looked beautiful to him. "You're the picture of health," he commented.

"I'm used to being outside on cold mornings. Remember, I help my dad on the farm."

He chuckled. "There's one good reason for wires: I got to listen in on all that you told Sven. And I must say, I wanted to hear more, just like he did!"

She smiled with a faraway look in her eyes. "It was a fairy-tale childhood followed by a disastrous time. I can't replace Sven's childhood, but I'm certainly going to do all I can to ensure he has a better life as an adult."

"Hear, hear," said Bruce as he raised his cup.

Bruce showed Katarina some of the sights she may have missed when she lived in New York. The highlight was Ground Zero. Katarina trembled when she considered her son was involved with such men as those who carried out this heinous crime. It scared her all over again.

Bruce knew what she was thinking. He covered her hand with his. "Don't worry; we're going to protect him and get him out of this."

Katarina looked up into his eyes and said, "I would like nothing better than to get Sven away from this city and all those evil men. I hope I can talk him into going back to the farm with me. When I told my dad about the FBI's visit and that I was coming here, he pledged his support for whatever I had to do. We've grown closer since I've become a woman; definitely not the girl who left home at eighteen."

"I can understand why he loves you."

Bruce thought, *I can't believe I just said that. It's too soon to even allude to anything so serious!*

Katarina never missed a beat and changed the subject. Bruce breathed a sigh of relief.

After a long day, Katarina begged off to go take a nap. After all the fresh air, Bruce needed one. They lay on their respective beds, both replaying the whole day, dissecting every conversation. Slowly, both slipped off into dreamland.

34.
New Friendships

Jim and Beth were sitting in Andy's luxurious living room. The sun was streaming in the window and it promised to be a beautiful day. Jim looked over at Beth and could tell she was in a comfortable zone, with her feet tucked up under her and a good book in her hands.

"Do you have anything you want to do today?" he asked. He had some paperwork but knew he wanted his lovely wife to be content.

"No, not really. I'm just enjoying not having any responsibilities," Beth said. "I'm glad Rebecca was able to return to her apartment. Even though she was no trouble, I did have to think what I would serve for meals. She called me yesterday to tell me they delivered her new crib. She's so excited."

I asked her if she would like to go to church with us tomorrow but she is going to Mass at her own church."

"That reminds me of something that's been going around in my mind," Jim said. "You know the young woman helping the FBI is in town and doesn't know many people. She's a Christian and I thought it would be nice to invite her to go to church with us and join us for lunch afterward. What do you think?"

"I'm good with it, honey. You just do the calling."

Jim called Bruce Foster, "Hey buddy. I wonder if you can give me Katarina's phone number? Beth and I would like to invite her to go to church with us."

Bruce was surprised at how considerate Jim was. Of course, Katarina had made it clear on the tape when talking with Sven that she was a Christian. He supplied the number and was ready to hang up when Jim said, "You're welcome to join us if you want."

Bruce hadn't been to church since his father died. He thought about Kararina and how pleased this would make her. "Sure, I'll join you. What church do you attend here?"

Jim told him where the church was located and asked if Bruce could pick up Katarina if she wanted to go.

He answered, "I'll go one better, I'll call her and tell her why I'm doing the calling instead of you. You can count on us coming unless I call you back."

Oh man, Bruce is over the top; hook, line, and sinker!

He turned to his wife, "Looks like Special Agent Foster has fallen for our Katarina Abadi. They *both* will be joining us at church, unless he calls back. I think I'll invite them to join us for lunch." He thought for a moment, "I guess I'd better call and make a reservation, which reminds me to ask Manny to pick us up in the morning. We'll catch a cab to the restaurant."

Beth was delighted about their plans for Sunday. She wasn't the only one; Katarina was thrilled to accept the invitation and looked forward to being with Bruce again.

On Sunday morning, Manny was waiting out front to pick up the Redmons. The couple got in the back seat, and Manny delivered them to the front of the church. Bruce and Katarina were waiting on the steps engrossed in one another. Jim said to Beth, "See what I mean?"

After the service was over, Jim asked if they could get a ride with Bruce to the restaurant. The FBI agent was pleased to accommodate them. When he was told where, he gulped; it was way too exclusive and expensive for his liking. Bruce's uneasiness disappeared when Jim explained they were to be his guests. Bruce started to argue, but Jim insisted.

Lunch was sumptuous. They were known for their famous Champagne brunch and good service, as well as their high prices. The group had a nice time and the ladies chatted while Bruce and Jim talked about one of their people who was recovering from a bad beating. When all was said and done, they were all on their way, with Bruce dropping the Redmons' at Andy's apartment.

Bruce turned to Katarina and explained he had to go into work; it was 1:30 pm. He apologized because he wanted to be with her but she was understanding and he dropped her at her hotel. She considered calling Sven, but was so tired after the stimulating morning, she laid down to take a nap.

Katarina's phone rang. It was Sven. "Mom, I don't have to clock in until five and wondered if I could come to your hotel room and chill out there?"

She was delighted. "Of course. I'm in my room now and I'll wait for you; I'm in room 321. How long do you think you'll be?"

"I should be there in 30 to 45 minutes."

Katarina luxuriated in the fact that her son chose to be with her this Sunday afternoon. It warmed her heart.

Within five minutes, the phone rang again.

A voice barked, "Why are you in New York?" There was no greeting, just the gruff question.

"Is that you, Ahmed?" she asked.

"Yes, it's me, and like I said, 'Why are you in New York?'"

"I thought it was high time I came to see my son. You've lied to him all these years and he thought I had abandoned him! Now it's my turn to tell him the truth."

"Yes, you did abandon him because you refused to honor your husband's wishes and become a Muslim. All of this could have been avoided if you had only done what you were told."

"Ahmed, you knew I was a Christian when you married me. What made you think I would leave my religion for yours? You didn't even follow your religion when I met you. It was months after we were married that you started attending the mosque. And that's when you changed into a monster."

The man was furious. "You never talked to me this way when we were married! I see a change for the worst in you since you've been out from under my leadership."

"I was *afraid* of you, Ahmed! Do you not remember how you used to beat me and how we went to the ER because you broke my arm? I can't believe your selective memory."

He seemed to settle into a quiet rage and spoke pointedly. "You will *NOT* mess up Sven's opportunity to prove himself a faithful Muslim. I won't let you. I want you to leave New York tomorrow."

She laughed. "Do you think you can dictate to me how to live my life? I'm not married to you, Ahmed. I divorced you years ago and I'm free of your tyranny. I shudder to think what you did to our son in the guise of caring for him. You never really loved him; *he* told me how he tried for years to win your approval but never did."

Ahmed started spewing hate words and Katarina very quietly hung up the phone.

She was shaking and called Bruce, relaying what her ex-husband had said to her. He told her not to open her door to anyone and he'd come over as soon as he was done at work.

The FBI was laying plans for the week. They had to intercept the explosives before they arrived at the Terminal. They needed agents to have eyes on every one of the men involved in the terror group. That meant Fred Houseman, Lockman, Ali Madur, Ralph Mercer, and the men who met at Lockman's house. They knew they wouldn't be able to arrest fringe people for lack of evidence, like Gofar, but the others would be rounded up by Friday afternoon.

Agent Townsley reported on the phone conversations they had intercepted from Ali Madur, which involved Houseman and included the deal made for the explosives. They also had plans to bring in the men who supposedly stole the dynamite. They knew their names and where they were working.

A sweet coup was that the FBI had an agent working in Houseman's mansion. She had been posing as a maid for months and had surreptitiously discovered his secret closet off his study. Once he was arrested, they would get a warrant and carefully dismantle the computer and were hopeful they would discover the names of more terrorists.

Bruce said he was most concerned about getting the information from Sven after Thursday night's meeting. He opened the floor for ideas. After hearing many ideas, they settled on the one where Sven would write down the plan and leave the paper in the glove compartment of his truck. In the wee hours of the morning, someone would retrieve it. If something unexpected happened, they'd go to Plan B: An agent was to follow each man who met at Lockman's house with the objective of stopping them from arriving at their homes with the explosives.

Ahmed Abadi called Jamaal to come get him. He was ready to carry out his plan. When his friend arrived, he saw the broken dishes in the kitchen. He could guess what had happened, his friend's temper got the best of him. "Are you sure about this, Ahmed? Do you think you can scare her enough to get her to leave?" Jamaal challenged.

"I know that woman better than anyone. She'll leave, you can be sure. I want you to wait for me in front of her hotel. It shouldn't take me more than fifteen or twenty minutes."

"Okay. If the cops make me move, I'll drive around the block and be right back."

Ahmed nodded, as he got into the cab.

Katarina was resting on her bed, with the TV turned down low. It was just a diversion as she didn't want to be alone after the upsetting conversation with Ahmed. She looked forward to Sven's arrival. When she heard the click of the lock, she was alarmed and sat up. When she saw Ahmed, the shocked look on her face pleased him. She started to get up and rush into the bathroom, but Ahmed was on her before she could get two steps.

"Get out of here," she screamed. Ahmed grabbed her by the arm and turned the TV volume up.

"It's a waste of time, Katarina. You can't get away from me now!" He threw her back on the bed and fell on her, slipping his hands around her throat. He thought, *It's a shame; such a beautiful woman, such a lovely throat.*

He started squeezing and she was flailing around, trying to get him to stop. She tore at his hands but to no avail. He was laughing at her fright but he kept his hands firmly in place. She started to gasp and he shouted, "I should have finished you off long ago! It would have made things so much easier."

Slowly Katarina stopped fighting. The madman kept laughing, but her body went limp. He seemed to snap out of it and looked with surprise at the young woman under him. She was dead; he didn't mean to kill her, just scare her. . . to death!

Jamaal didn't have to move his car. A guest from the hotel tried to engage him, but he said he was waiting for someone. He waited patiently and was surprised when Ahmed came out so soon. He looked frightened and jumped in the cab and told Jamaal to move quickly.

As he pealed off, he asked, "What happened, Ahmed? You look like you've seen a ghost."

"There's only one thing you need to know, Jamaal. If anyone asks you, I've been with you the whole afternoon." He slammed his hand down on the dash and Jamaal saw the scratches on his hands. "That stupid woman!" He would say no more.

Bruce called Katarina several times after he concluded his meeting. "Maybe she's in the bathroom." He tried two more times but no answer. Finally, he became concerned and drove to the hotel. He asked the manager to ring the phone in the room; no answer. He showed his badge and asked the manager to go up to the room with him. When the door was opened, Bruce knew just by looking at Katarina, that she'd been assaulted. He rushed over and felt for a pulse; nothing. He couldn't believe it. This beautiful woman that he was falling in love with was dead! He told the manager to call the police and he sat down on the chair with his head in his hands.

Bruce got it together and called Jim. He croaked, "Jim. . ."

"What is it, Bruce? Are you in trouble?"

"No, not me. Katarina has been murdered. Can you come right away? I'm in her hotel room."

"Sure, buddy. Have you called the police yet?"

"I told the manager to call for me. I'm just sitting here looking at her remembering our. . ." He started to cry.

Jim hung up and called Bob Stevens explaining briefly what had happened and where he was headed. Bob promised to meet him at the Nobel.

When Jim grabbed his coat, Beth came out of the bedroom and asked him what in the world was going on. He sat down on the sofa, drawing her close. "Katarina has been murdered. Bruce just called and he wants me to come right away."

Beth was too shocked for words. Finally when she could speak, she said, "You can't mean that beautiful young woman who went to church with us and then to lunch is dead, do you?"

He nodded, and the tears welled up in his wife's eyes. She asked if he wanted her to come with him but he said no; he'd call her later when he had some information. Jim grabbed the keys to Manny's truck parked in the parking garage and left calling over his shoulder, "Call Manny and tell him where I'm going and why."

35.
Tragedy

All the way to the hotel, Jim's thoughts ran in many directions. Who? When? How? Was there a struggle? Where was she? He parked in a No Parking zone and could have cared less. When he exited the truck, Bob Stevens was hopping out of a squad car. They both rushed in, Bob showing his I.D. and Jim following as the manager took them up to Room 321.

Bruce was standing in the hall near the doorway. He was giving instructions to another agent. The man moved away and Bob and Jim approached. Jim put his hand on his friend's shoulder. This brought Bruce close to tears so Jim moved away.

"Tell us what happened," encouraged Bob.

Bruce told him how he had brought Katarina back from church and was supposed to call her when he was through with his meeting. He spoke to her briefly during one of his breaks but there was no indication she was in trouble. When he called her to tell her he was on his way, he received no answer. He called several times with no luck; he jumped in his car and tore over here. He had a feeling of misgiving when she didn't answer the phone in the room. He and the manager finally came up to her room and opened the door. While trying to reign in his emotions, Bruce relayed what he saw; how he called Jim, the FBI, and how the police unit just arrived before Jim and Bob Stevens. The FBI was already on the scene.

Jim spoke up and told Bruce he had called Bob immediately and how they had both arrived at the same time.

Just then, Bruce's cell rang and he listened a moment. Frantically he whirled around toward the elevator. The doors opened and Sven bounded out. "Where is she? Where's my mom?" he yelled.

Bruce went to him and held him, trying to keep him from entering the room. "Sven, Sven. Listen to me. Come back to the elevators and let's sit down. I need to talk to you."

By this time, men were stringing yellow tape across the hall leading up to the room. Some guests were looking out their doors, whispering to one another. Bob Stevens said, "Would everyone please go back into their rooms. There's been an accident and we could work more efficiently if you would all close your doors." They grudgingly did what they were told.

The elevator doors opened and the ME exited followed by an assistant with a stretcher.

Sven's eyes opened wide. "He killed her, didn't he? I just knew he couldn't stand the thought of our being together. He's a madman." He started to weep. Bruce held the young man and let him cry. "I just got her back and he took her away, again!" he moaned. He wrenched out of Bruce's grasp. "I'm going to kill that s.o.b."

Bruce asked him to sit down, then knelt down on his haunches in front of the young man. He looked him straight in the eye and asked, "We don't have the evidence against him yet, Sven, but I agree with you that it's fairly certain your father did this. Do you want to make Ahmed pay?"

Sven gained some control and answered. "More than anything."

"Then let's do it together; I think I want him as bad as you do."

The ME did his job and they wheeled Katarina's draped body out of the room. Before they wheeled her out, Bruce moved Sven into an empty room provided by the hotel. The detectives continued to process the scene and when they were done, Bruce asked Sven if he wanted to collect her things.

"If you'd take them for me until this is finished, I'd appreciate it. I have nowhere to store them." He looked solemn and inquired, "Do you know how I can contact my grandfather?"

Bruce was surprised. All of a sudden Sven wasn't Ahmed's son, but Katarina's son; and her father was no longer a stranger but his grandfather. "I can get that number for you, Sven. When you call him, I'll be right here for moral support."

Jim suggested Sven call Gofar and tell him he got a stomach virus; he wouldn't be able to come to work this evening and would he explain to his boss. Gofar agreed to deliver the message.

Jim spoke quietly to Sven telling him he would be glad to provide plane fare for his grandfather to come to New York if he needed it. But he suggested Sven wait until the terrorist threat was over before he called him. Sven agreed, but he hated having to wait; he felt his grandfather deserved to know now!

Jim took Sven to Andy's apartment. He knew Beth was a very compassionate woman and would reach out to Sven like a son. Jim called and gave Beth a heads-up answering her questions as best he could. It was inconceivable the young man had lost his mom right after he was reunited with her again. She started preparing a light supper; then she prayed.

The two men entered the apartment and Sven was surprised at the opulence of the place. But the minute Beth entered the room, his defenses went down and she gathered him into her arms. He was overwhelmed; he kept thinking of all that he had missed because his father had a *control* issue. These strangers really cared!

They talked over supper and then the two guys went into the living room for a cup of coffee while Beth cleaned up the kitchen. Sven shared his doubts about the direction his mosque was taking. None of it really made any sense to him. Jim asked him why he became a member if he didn't really believe any of it. Sven was thoughtful; "I guess I was still trying to gain my father's approval. He was fanatical about my being a part of the group, of belonging!"

Jim inquired, "Didn't you think killing all those people was wrong?"

"You don't seem to understand the depth of their brainwashing. I started *believing* it was for the greater good to wipe out as many Americans as possible. . . the infidels."

"When did you start thinking differently?"

"When I was with my mother and she showed me so much love, I had a hard time believing this was the infidel that my father hated with every fiber of his being. There was a stirring within me that I can't explain. I guess the five years she had me made a difference in my core."

Jim told Sven he needed to be real smart; "you'll have to put on an Academy Award appearance. You must not let your father know that you're aware of your mother's death. You'll get so much more information by allowing him to do most of the talking."

Sven considered this. "My father likes everyone to listen to him. He thinks he's king."

"So you let him be king tonight, and every night until your meeting with Lockman."

"When you go in tonight, you tell your dad you spent the night in the bathroom with a stomach virus. He doesn't have to know which bathroom. This is just in case Gofar puts his two cents worth in. Then you ask him what *he* did today. . .an innocent question. See what he says and remember every word. Then you yawn and tell him you are worn out and are going to bed. He'll be delighted because he's scared to death what you'll do when you find out about your mother."

Jim looked at the young man and quietly laid out a scenario for him. "You know Sven, think of the people the terrorists are planning to kill. They all have someone in their lives who care for them; just like you loved your mother and she loved you. Think of the broken hearts when they discover that loved one has been killed. You now can relate! I'm so thankful you decided to abandon those who are planning this chilling attack. I feel like your mother's visit to New York to try to save you from them was successful. She'd be thrilled that her death wasn't in vain."

Sven went home that night and did exactly as Jim had told him. He flopped down on the sofa, interrupting his father's show. He told him about his stomach virus and then said, "I went to prayer today; not as many people there as usual." he said casually.

Ahmed looked up with interest, "Why today?" he asked.

Sven shrugged his shoulders, "No reason, I guess. Just seemed to be the thing to do with so much happening this week for the faithful."

Ahmed was very pleased. He made no comment.

Sven got up for a cold drink, purposely not looking at his father when he returned to the living room. "Funny thing. I've called my mother several times but there was no answer. She told me she wanted to spend some time with me today, but I never heard from her."

Ahmed fidgeted in his chair, "Maybe she decided to go home early."

"Without saying goodbye? No way. She told me she came all this way to be with *me.*"

The father became irritated, "Well how would *I* know. I couldn't figure that silly woman out when I was married to her; how would I know why she's done something now?"

"No reason; I was just thinking out loud." He went to bed.

36.
Academy Award

On Monday morning, Ahmed was jittery. He had checked the newspaper but saw nothing about a dead woman found at the Nobel Hotel. He thought, *Surely someone has discovered Katarina's body by now. Probably the Housekeeping staff.* He had a dark thought, *Maybe that guy she was with on Saturday night found her body and has been blamed for her death.* The thought made him smile.

That same morning, Sven pretended to sleep in. He couldn't bear to be around his father pretending everything was okay. As soon as he heard his father leave the apartment, he went in and took a shower and then sat down at the kitchen table with a cup of coffee. The night before seemed like a dream to him, a bad dream. He decided to call Bruce Foster like he'd been asked.
"This is Sven."
"Are you okay, son?"
"I guess I'm okay for the moment. It comes and goes."
"Jim told me how he advised you last night. How did it go with your father?" Bruce inquired.
"It was easy and he never suspected I knew anything. I'm really wondering if I can pull this off three more days."
"Sure you can. I'll have Jim talk you through some possible developments. What he said to you last night seemed to work."
"Yeah. I think that'd be good. What do you want me to do today?"
"Absolutely nothing out of the ordinary. Do what you usually do and talk with people naturally. Do you attend prayer at the mosque?"
"Yes. I'm not as regular as my father would have me be, but I go."
"Then today you go like nothing has happened."

Bruce talked with as many hotel employees as possible. The

manager said he saw a man come in around the time of death but didn't pay close attention because he went right to the elevators; he assumed he was a guest.

The agent thanked him and asked him to let him know if he thought of anything else. As the guy started to do some work, he looked Bruce's way saying, "You know, a couple of our guests were going out yesterday afternoon and there was a cab at the door. They decided not to walk and tried to hire the cabbie to take them. He said he was waiting for a party. Funny thing, I usually call cabs for our guests but this cab obviously had been called by someone else."

Bruce wasn't one to believe in coincidences. "Do you recall anything about the cab? Like a company name or color?"

"It was orange and I think it was a Ford; that's all I remember."

Bruce thanked the man and went over to a computer area off the lobby. He called the office and put someone on the hunt for an orange Ford cab that had been called to the Nobel Hotel on Sunday afternoon. When the agent got back with Bruce, it was a dead-end. What was so strange, none of the companies had received a call for a cab at the Nobel Hotel.

Jim brought Manny up to date on Sunday's happenings. Manny was shocked to say the least.

Jim called Bruce to hear his thoughts about having a meeting with Bob Stevens and Manny regarding the entire case. He felt the homicide, which was Bob's department, and the truth that Andy was alive should be shared. They all had to trust someone sooner or later and having more people brainstorming together would probably be helpful. Bruce agreed. They were going to meet at Andy's apartment that afternoon with the possibility of meeting at FBI headquarters later.

All the lawmen, including Manny, sat down ready to brainstorm as had been suggested. Jim opened the discussion.

"First of all, Bruce, I think it's time to enlighten everyone about Andy."

It was an understatement that everyone was shocked. Bob Stevens threw Jim a dirty look and Jim looked innocent and shrugged his shoulders. Bruce smiled and said, "It was all my fault, Bob. I swore Jim to secrecy."

The information about Fred Houseman and his gallery was shared. Jim and Bob knew most of it, but they told everything in hopes that the information might trigger something new.

Bruce told the group all they knew about Houseman and his minions. They all were interested in what the FBI had planned for the meeting at Lockman's. Bruce told them about their plans.

Manny spoke up. "No way would I take a chance even one man could slip through your net. All it would take would be for one bomb to go off and we'd have panic; plus death and destruction."

"You're absolutely right. I think something must be done as soon as the crew leaves Lockman's," Jim added.

Bruce seemed deep in thought. "I'd like to figure out a way to remove Sven from the group after they're all taken to headquarters. We must initially treat him like all the others. Even if we think we've got them all, there are people on the fringes we aren't aware of and they would want vengeance. After investigating, they might find out that Sven was talking to his mother and who knows what all." Everyone nodded their agreement.

"Since we don't know what Lockman's going to tell them, we're at a loss. They could keep all the bombs and hand them out individually on Friday morning. A lot can happen we don't know about." Bruce was thoughtful, "And we aren't even sure when they plan to set them off. There are so many unknowns!"

Bob asked, "Did you say you have an agent assigned to all the men attending the meeting?"

"Yes. But until Thursday night we aren't even sure which one will be chosen to set the timer or make arrangements for the explosion. Sven was adamant that this wasn't a suicide mission. I contend he may not know what the bosses planned, so we're not sure about anything until Thursday night."

Bob Stevens asked if Sven could wear a wire. Bruce told him they couldn't chance it in case there was suspicion and all the men would be searched. He reminded them this was a huge mission. Bob asked "Is there some other way he could record the meeting?"

Bruce sat thinking. "I know everyone thinks we have things available like you see in the movies, but if they do, I'm not aware of it. One thing's for sure, I'll ask."

Jim reiterated that through Sven they knew the explosion was to take place on Friday the 13th. "Now if I were planning an attack at the terminal on Friday, I think I would pick a prime travel time in order to make a statement." Everyone nodded. "And someone told Sven it was perfect he already worked at the restaurant. He clocks in around four for his shift; which makes me think he'll have something to do with planting his device in the restaurant." Nods again.

"Those are good conjectures, Jim, but we can't be sure."

"Which is why you need to have some way for Sven to record that meeting!" retorted Jim.

37.
Solutions

When Bruce returned to headquarters, he talked with his agents about trying to prove that Ahmed Abadi was involved in Katarina's death. There was no mystery about how he found out where she was staying. Innocently, Sven had told his father.

All the agents had met Katarina and were more than ready to help catch her killer. One of the agents shared that there wasn't one fingerprint in the hotel room. He said even the doorknob was wiped clean.

Bruce suggested he try to get a full description of the man seen entering shortly before her death. "The manager told me he didn't pay any attention because he thought the man was a guest. But we all know there are ways to retrieve information from a person that thinks they didn't see anything."

He then asked another agent to try to find out what companies had orange cabs; which ought to be easier because most were yellow. He also needed to know what cabs were on the streets that day.

While the men sat around the table, Bruce called Sven. "Are you alone?"

"Yes. I'm on my way home from work. I might lose you in the subway. Can I call. . ." Sven lost him.

After an impatient lull, Sven called back. "Sorry about that. What's up?"

"I need to ask you some questions about Lockman. We've had his house under surveillance for some time now and we've never seen a woman going in or out. Is Lockman married, or have children?"

"No. He lives alone and prides himself that he isn't burdened by a 'dumb female'.

He definitely has no respect for women."

Bruce was happy *that* problem was resolved. "Sven, do you know if he records or videos your meetings?"

"No, not that I'm aware. I DO know he has a burglar alarm system; I've seen the pad inside his front door."

"Where does Lockman hold the meetings?"

"In his living room; we've always met there. It's an old house and I don't think the basement is finished."

"Thanks, Sven. As far as your mother's murder is concerned, I'm sorry to report we have no new information but we're working on it." The young man hung up.

Jim called Bruce the following morning. "Bruce, I have an idea and I wanted to run it by you. Manny's here and I have you on speaker."

"That's funny, but I have an idea, too."

"You first," replied Jim.

"Our hands are tied regarding recording, videoing, etcetera. The federal government wants to protect its innocent citizens. I understand that, but when you have a gut feeling about a man, you don't want your hands tied."

Jim interrupted, "And you want me to do what you can't do. Isn't that right?"

Bruce was surprised. "We seem to be on the same page again."

Manny rolled his eyes, "You two are *twins* when it comes to solving a case."

"What were you going to suggest, Bruce."

"Why don't you just tell me what you have planned," the man said with a smirk.

Jim offered, "I'll need some information about Lockman's hours, because I think we can plant a device in his living room or somewhere he'll never check. We *need* a recording of that meeting on Thursday."

"I wholeheartedly agree. Why don't you come here and we'll arrange it." He paused, "You know of course that if this blows up in our faces, I never knew anything about it."

Jim grinned, "I would expect nothing less."

The two had it all arranged thirty minutes after Jim arrived at FBI Headquarters. He called Sven and asked him if he knew if Lockman went home during the day. Sven had no idea, but he knew Lockman marched to Houseman's drum and he got the impression he seemed to be a strict boss.

After hanging up with Sven, Jim and Manny mapped their strategy. Bruce agreed to have a couple of agents shadow them and give them a heads up if Lockman's car appeared. Jim was grateful to have backup. Bruce also supplied them with blue servicemen jumpsuits to wear, in case someone got nosy.

Around 1:45 pm, Manny and Jim circled Lockman's block several times. The neighborhood seemed devoid of activity. When they realized there was an alley behind the row of homes, Manny drove into it and parked his pick-up a couple of houses down from Lockman's. Manny had a clip board with him and they wore ball caps; both men looked like servicemen. They peered into the kitchen window to check it out but realized there was no way to enter there.

As they carefully did a perimeter search, they realized all entries were tied into the alarm system. As Jim was walking on the side of the house, he noticed a boarded up window; it looked like an old coal shoot. He motioned to Manny and they went to work prying the board off; it was tedious work. After removing it, they carefully set it aside and slipped into the basement. It was filthy with old coal dust. They both sat on the basement steps and slipped shoe covers over their shoes. Bruce thought of everything.

After stealthily climbing the stairs, they were surprised to find the door locked to the first floor. Jim examined it and Manny nudged him aside. With ease, he had the door unlocked quickly. Jim whispered, "You'll have to teach me that trick."

They entered the kitchen from the basement and could tell Lockman didn't believe in a clean kitchen. They saw pots and pans that were stacked in the sink and they obviously had been there for days. The wastebasket was spilling over with dirty paper products. The two men did a quick search to check for cameras. None.

Just off the kitchen was a small dining room. Beyond it was the living room, which was definitely not going to be photographed for an interior design magazine. It had an old brown sofa, a couple of ancient stuffed chairs, a beat up coffee table and two end tables piled with old newspapers and junk mail. Most importantly, a huge TV was mounted on the wall. There were old drapes hanging at the windows. They noticed the key pad for the alarm inside the front door but no cameras so far.

Leading from the front door was a small hallway straight ahead. There were two small bedrooms and they could see the bathroom at the end of the hall. They surmised the first bedroom was where

Lockman slept; the other one was locked. Manny went to work again and had it opened in moments. This was the neatest room in the house, with a desk, a chair and a computer. Jim quickly texted Bruce telling him of their find.

Bruce was glad they found it but directed them to lock the door again and disregard. They'd have agents check it out later.

The two went back into the living room and tried to figure out the best place to plant the bug. They came to the conclusion, after a process of elimination: don't place it near the TV because he may turn it on when he comes in from work, not on the drapery rod because he'd probably close them before the meeting, not on the lamps because they were too obvious in case Lockman did a sweep of the room. They finally decided to plant one on the back side of the front leg of the sofa. It was totally hidden and they felt good about it. They texted Bruce and told him it was in place and to check it out from his end.

Jim went over to the doorway into the living room and spoke softly. Manny stood in the dining room doorway and said a few words. Then Jim stood behind one of the chairs and spoke. Bruce texted them they picked up every word from every location. He asked them to take the extra bug and hide it in Lockman's office. Manny reentered the room and placed a bug on the back leg of the desk. It, too, was totally inconspicuous. He locked the room and the two left the way they had come in. Getting out was much more difficult than *dropping* in. The board was put back in place, and the two *servicemen* left the premises.

When the truck rounded the corner, Jim fist-bumped Manny. "Way to go, partner."

When Jim arrived home that evening, he decided to give Philip Warren a call with an update on the case. He purposely didn't tell him Andy was alive as he thought it would be more meaningful if he told him the news when he could hand the phone over to Andy.

He mainly told Philip about the situation with the FBI and Sven's involvement. The elderly man was satisfied.

38.
Case Solved

The Medical Examiner called Bruce with his report. He said Katarina had obviously fought her attacker because they found DNA under her fingernails. Bruce thought, *Ahmed thought he was so smart in wiping off the doorknob and making sure he left no evidence, but the best evidence was unseen!* This was great news. He'd call Sven first; the young man deserved to be the first to hear.

When he dialed Sven's number, he realized he might be at work but he answered on the first ring. "Hello."

"Sven, it's Bruce. Can you talk a minute?"

"Yes. No one has sat at my tables yet; it's early." The young man was standing in a doorway waiting.

"I just wanted you to know that the Medical Examiner just called and told us that your mother didn't go down without a fight. They found DNA under her fingernails!"

"That's great! Now what?"

Bruce asked, "Could you find out if your father has any scratches on his hands or forearms?"

"That's easy. I'll get up before he goes to work."

"Great. Just let me know as soon as you can. You have my cell number and can call at any hour."

"Okay. Do you have any other evidence against him?"

Bruce decided to share it all; after all, it *was* Sven's mother and, personally speaking, it was *his* Katarina. "We've got some leads but can't seem to find the cab that was parked outside the hotel at the time of Katarina's death."

Sven's heart skipped a beat. "A CAB," he shouted. A couple of waiters turned to look at him, and he lowered his voice. "My father's best friend is a cab driver! His name is Jamaal and he does pretty much what my father tells him."

Bruce had a shiver go down his back. He couldn't believe this, the information had fallen into his lap. *Thank You, God!* he thought. "Do you know the name of the company he works for?"

Sven gave him the information and said his first customers had come in and he had to go. He promised to call Bruce the minute he could check his father's hands.

Bruce called his agent who was investigating the cab companies. "The information we've been looking for was just dropped into my lap!" He told Jim the name of the company and asked him to take a partner and go to the their offices. He wanted all the information they could get on a guy named Jamaal who worked there.

His next call was to Jim. He reported what Sven had told him and how some of his agents were on their way to check out the cab company. "I just found out from the Medical Examiner that DNA was found under Katarina's fingernails. Sven is going to check out his father's hands. Looks like things are perking right along."

"Way to go, Bruce. I'm meeting with Sven in the morning around ten. He's coming over here if you want a free cup of coffee."

"I'll be there. And you might want to ask Bob and Manny. Bob's got some information about Mercer that he wants to share and not on the phone. I'm curious."

He paused a moment, "Andy is not being a good patient. In fact, he's *im*patient and wants out of there. What do you say we run out there and see him tonight?"

Jim agreed and they set a time. When he hung up, he called the guys to come to the apartment at ten the next morning.

Ralph Mercer left the precinct for a break. He seldom left the building, but he needed to make a phone call away from curious ears. He ducked into a familiar diner and chose a seat in the back.

A red-headed waitress approached. "Hey stranger, you haven't been in for a long time. What can I get you?" The waitress had been attracted to Ralph from the first time he came in, and he knew it. He wasn't married and he saw her checking out his ring finger.

"Just bring me coffee and a donut, Rosemary."

The waitress wrote down his order, gave him a cute wink, and left the table. He figured he'd better wait for his food; he didn't want to be interrupted.

After his order arrived, Ralph dialed. His call was answered and he responded, "This is Ralph, sorry for the late hour. I needed to give you the latest because something's going on and I haven't been successful in finding out what." He listened to the response and continued, "After the cell phone fiasco, and the friend of the dead guy picked it up, our lead detective has been snooping around asking questions. I asked the guy who goes off before me if he'd stay a little later for me last night. He has always been friendly about it before, but last night he was abrupt and refused. It got my attention. I mentioned it to my buddy who is with a patrol unit and he said someone was nosing around about him. I felt like I needed to report this to you even though it didn't seem like much." After being praised for his due diligence, Mercer hung up and enjoyed his donut and coffee.

Lockman called Mr. Houseman immediately. He felt like it wouldn't be wise to wait 'til morning; the boss wouldn't be pleased. He related the call from Mercer, and added, "I think we ought to be extra careful. Something doesn't smell right."

Houseman agreed. They both had a hard time going to sleep. The thought of someone being onto them was disconcerting, to say the least. First thing in the morning, the boss planned to call Ali Madur. He decided to have the explosives delivered directly to Lockman's house instead of his warehouse. He called Lockman back about the change.

Jim waited downstairs for Bruce to pick him up. It was after nine o'clock and bitter cold. The two talked about the case all the way to the safe house. Before they entered Andy's room, Mandy gave them a warning by rolling her eyes. They saw Andy sitting in a recliner watching TV. When he saw the men, he released the lever and the foot rest came crashing down.

"It's about time you two showed up! I've been crawling the walls around here. I feel fine and the doctor said I was okay. . .so when do I get to get outta' here?"

Jim chuckled, "Same old Andy; impatient as usual."

"You got that right! *You* try laying around here for weeks."

"Calm down, buddy. We've come to bring you up to speed." Between the two of them, they shared with Andy all that was going on with the case.

He glanced at Bruce, "I'm sorry about the woman, Bruce. That's one tough break." Then he looked at Jim, "What's happening with Rebecca?"

"She's still pregnant," Jim said.

"If I weren't so weak, I'd slug you," he said half in jest.

Bruce decided they'd enjoyed enough levity at Andy's expense. "I know you want to go home, Andy. But after hearing what's been going on, if they found out you were still alive, that would change everything. We don't want anything to rock the boat. Let's allow it to play out and I promise you we'll try to get you out of here on Saturday morning."

"Having a date to look forward to is something!" He changed gears. "How are we going to tell Rebecca? I don't want to shock her so much that it causes problems with the pregnancy. I've had a lot of time to think about this and I'd like to propose to her and give her a ring *before* she tells me. That would help a lot."

"Let me think about it, Andy. I think it's time to bring Beth in on the secret. She always has great ideas about matters of the heart."

After another fifteen minutes of visiting, the two men left. Andy called out, "See you Saturday morning."

Sven called Bruce later that night. He'd seen his father in the kitchen when he got home from work. The man was in his pajama bottoms and a tee shirt and the scratches were evident. When Sven went to bed, he texted Bruce with the news that his father had scratches on one forearm and both hands. He told him it made him sick *and* mad. He had to leave the room before he jumped him.

Bruce replied, "Okay Sven, I understand. You just be cool. I'll talk to you at Jim's tomorrow."

Jim got home quite late and didn't want to open a can of worms at that hour. He slept fitfully and rose early, as usual. Beth was up and had the coffee going.

He slipped up behind her, encircling her waist. "Hey honey. Can we talk?"

Beth looked at him askance. "If you need to ask, then this must be something important."

Jim led her to the counter stools. "Do you remember when Bruce Foster came here for the first time? He asked me to take a ride with him but swore me to secrecy about where we were going."

"I vaguely remember. I was already in bed."

He cleared his throat. "Well, he took me to see Andy!"

"He WHAT?"

"You heard me. Andy is alive." He took her hands in his. "For his own protection, he's under a doctor's care in a safe house outside of Manhattan. Andy was in bad shape the first time I saw him, but he's been healing quickly. Our subsequent visits surprised us. He can walk now, and is as irritable as a wet hen."

Beth was still reeling. She couldn't even think of a question to ask.

"After Rebecca stumbled on those men in her apartment, I knew Andy would have my head if I didn't tell him. He then insisted we take him to the hospital to see her. It was late at night and we figured she would be asleep." Jim finished telling his wife the story about Andy's visit.

"Do you want to hear something funny?" Beth asked. "Rebecca thought she dreamed Andy had come into her room."

Jim chuckled. "And he did, but drew back when her eyes fluttered open. She immediately closed them and we thought we were scot-free."

She had a thoughtful look on her face, "What was in the casket?"

"I guess rocks." He continued on without hesitation. "Now this is Andy's thinking: He'd like to propose to her before she tells him she's pregnant. And we both know he's already bought the ring. How can we do this?" He glanced at her with a smile, "I told him this was right up your alley."

39.
Suspicion

Fred Houseman called Ali Madur the following morning. "Ali, this is Houseman. There's been a change of plans; I want you to deliver the explosives to Lockman's house on Thursday night." Ali was full of questions but Houseman cut him off. "I don't want to discuss it now. I'm in charge of this operation and when or what I do with it is none of your concern."

When Lockman got home that day, he did a thorough search of his house. He could not tell anyone had come in but he knew the authorities could find a way if they wanted. His alarm hadn't been tripped and all the doors were locked; including the door to the basement. When he was satisfied, he reported his findings to Houseman. "I think everything is okay; doesn't appear that anyone has entered my place."

"Good. Have you done a thorough investigation of the men you've chosen?"

"Yes. There's only one I feel might be suspect, and that's Ahmed Abadi's son, Sven. His father pushed him on me, so I checked him out and he seemed alright. He hasn't been a regular at the mosque until the last couple years. His mother abandoned them when Sven was little, so he's only half Arab; his mother is Norwegian. He has his mother's blue eyes and I thought this would benefit us since he doesn't look like a brother."

"Tell me about his father; I have only seen Ahmed a few times at the mosque." Houseman inquired.

"Ahmed is fanatical about his faith and would do anything radical for the cause."

Houseman murmured, "Too bad Ahmed doesn't have the job at the restaurant." He paused, thinking. "Let's take another look at this Sven Abadi. How old is he?"

"Around 24. He runs around with a couple of guys in our community."

"Can you talk to any of them without raising a red flag?"

Lockman paused to think about it. "Yes, I believe I can talk with the guy he works with. He helped Sven get the job at the restaurant. His name is Gofar Hakimi."

"Then do it today. We don't want any surprises!"

Houseman walked into the breakfast room of his opulent home. His wife and two kids were seated at the table enjoying cereal and fresh fruit. "Good morning," he said pleasantly.

"Good morning, father," the children said dutifully.

He smiled at his beautiful family. "Dahlia, I've been thinking; it would be a wonderful time for us to take a much-needed family vacation."

Dahlia looked at him as if he were speaking in another language. They had *never* taken a family vacation, but she wasn't about to argue.

"I think it would be a wonderful time to visit Cuba. They have just opened their borders to American citizens and I understand it is a beautiful country. It will be warm and lovely and I have a place in mind. One of my business associates has a nice villa outside of Havana he would let us use. It comes with servants, has a pool, and horses." His son's eyes perked up and he couldn't help but laugh at the boy's interest. "Yes, son, horses you can *ride!*"

Dahlia didn't know what was happening but she knew Fred well enough to know when he made *wonderful* plans for his family it usually meant it was for *his* best interests. She asked, "When are we leaving, and will you make the arrangements?"

He answered her question with a nagging thought she didn't trust his motives. "I plan to make the arrangements now but wanted to tell you first. If all works out, you should be on the plane by tomorrow morning. Does a day give you enough time to get ready?"

"Are you saying that you won't be coming with us?"

"Not tomorrow, as I have a big business meeting in the evening to prepare for a show and auction on Friday night. I plan to leave for Cuba on Saturday morning. Jose can pack for me so you will have nothing to do but pack for you and the children."

She was beginning to get excited, but with a pout said, "I would have liked to shop before I go. I understand Cuba doesn't have many high-end boutiques yet."

He patted her on the shoulder, "You have two closets full of clothes, Dahlia. Surely you have enough swimsuits and summer dresses for this trip without shopping!"

She acquiesced.

Bruce and his team of agents were hard at work by seven in the morning. He heard reports from the other agencies involved in the case. The chatter they had been hearing was miniscule. He wondered why. The agents in Paris had some interesting information; a number of known radical Muslims had been seen frequenting the antique store. They were on alert in case a like-situation was planned for Paris. He had a crack team ready to enter Lockman's house and scrub his computer the minute they got the go-ahead. They had the same plan for Houseman's home.

The group gathered around the conference table and were instructed to be on their toes on Thursday evening. If all went according to plan, they would be rounding up all the men involved in the attack. They were told about the bugged living room and computer room at Lockman's house.

Bruce's phone rang. He heard that Houseman had just ordered his plane to be prepared to leave for Cuba. His wife and children would be going without him.

All of the group arrived but Sven. They all waited on the young man before starting the meeting. When he arrived, Jim told them about how he and Manny got into Lockman's house and planted the bugs.

Sven said, "Isn't that illegal?"

Jim shrugged his shoulders. "I'm willing to take responsibility if need be." Manny gave his assent for his part in it also. Jim added with assurance, "Just so you understand, the FBI had no part in this."

Bruce told them about the scratch's on Ahmed's hands and forearm and how Sven had called him to confirm the fact. He told them about how they had picked up Jamaal early this morning for questioning. Then Bruce explained he had two agents shadowing Ahmed. Even though they had enough evidence to arrest him, they didn't want to tip their hand before the take-down of the group. Bob Stevens nodded his assent.

Sven spoke, "It isn't soon enough for me!" He saw the concern on Jim's face. "Don't worry, I'll keep my cool."

Bruce told them they had heard the call between Lockman and Houseman. "Lockman asked why the delivery of the explosives was to be his house instead of the warehouse."

He turned to Sven, "There was talk concerning you. I think

they're suspicious and Lockman gave a clear description of how he brought you in as one of the chosen group. He was asked about your father and Lockman described him as a radical fanatic. Also, Lockman said he'd check you out with a guy named Gofar Hakimi."

Sven was shocked. "This is getting dicey, but no problem. I don't think Gofar has any idea about my early childhood *or* my Christian mother, and I sure didn't tell him she was in town."

Jim spoke up, "You watch your back, Sven. These people don't value life and would kill you in a heartbeat." The young man nodded in agreement.

While the FBI spent the rest of the day getting things in place for Thursday, Jim listened to Beth's ideas for getting Andy and Rebecca together. Meanwhile, Bob Stevens went back to headquarters to thwart Mercer and prepare for the FBI to arrest him.

Sven went to work, watching Gofar with interest. His friend never interacted with him and he thought, *I guess Lockman hasn't spoken to him yet.* He went home after his shift and was glad his father was already in bed. In his remembrance, this was one night that he barely slept.

40.
Final Instructions

Morning dawned and it promised to be a warm, sunny day for mid-March. As the morning progressed, the weather report turned out to be true.

Around 11:30, there was a knock at Gofar's door. He had just finished taking a shower and only had time to pull on his pants. With a towel draped around his shoulders, he opened the door. His heart dropped into his belly; for there stood the ominous Lockman.

"I need to talk to you," the visitor said, as he pushed himself into the room. "It'll only take a moment." Gofar motioned to a chair and he sat on the sofa facing the man.

"I think you are aware of some big plans our community is planning for this week." It wasn't a question; but a statement.

Gofar nodded, but quickly added, "But I don't know what or when."

Lockman chose his words carefully. "We have big plans for one of your friends. He is climbing the ladder to become a very valuable addition to our organization. I'm talking about Sven Abadi." He watched the young man for any sign of angst but there was no change in expression. "Is there anything helpful you can tell me about Sven?"

"I met him a couple years ago when he started coming to the Mosque. We had fun together and I'd say we're pretty good friends. I knew he was looking for a job and heard that the restaurant where I work was hiring. He got a job. End of story."

"Is he a good worker? I heard he got promoted to waiter pretty quickly. Is that about right?"

"Yeah. He's a good worker and quick." Gofar was quick to add, "But *I'm* not interested in beating my brains out for a job as a waiter."

Lockman decided to ask one more question. "Do you think he is a good Muslim and would do just about anything for his faith?"

Gofar thought a moment before answering. "I think he'd be

considered a good Muslim but I don't know anything beyond that. We've never talked about it."

Lockman stood, satisfied he'd gotten what he had come for. "Thanks, Gofar. You were a big help. I'll remember that."

Gofar suddenly felt important.

Gofar called Sven and asked him if he wanted to play some computer games. Sven declined but said he'd be interested in going out for lunch. The two made arrangements to meet at a joint in their area around two.

Sven thought, *Lockman has talked to Gofar. He can't wait to tell me the big man sought him out for information.*

The two met as arranged, and it didn't take Gofar long to report word for word all that Lockman had said. He added, "I guess they figured I was especially important to give them the information they wanted."

Sven felt sorry for Gofar's feelings of inferiority. He enthusiastically replied, "Way to go, man. You knew exactly what to say to put a favorable light on me. I wonder what plans they have for me?" he asked innocently.

"I have no idea. Just remember who your friends are when you get to the top," he said with a laugh.

Gofar changed directions, "Do you go in at four today? Thought we'd do something after work."

"I'm off this evening. I have a pile of laundry to do then I thought I'd watch TV and turn in early."

Bob Stevens made an appointment with Ralph Mercer's boss. They were going to meet on Friday and Bob prepared what he was going to say. By then this fiasco should be over

Bruce instructed every team about their responsibilities. He had charge of more agents than he had ever directed in his career. Some of the agents were already in place. Bruce thought it would be good to have strange vehicles in place long before people returned home from work. He had found out that practically every adult that lived in the neighborhood had a job outside of their home. The earliest home arrival would be four o'clock.

Jim and Beth had a long conversation regarding Andy and Rebecca. Beth had finally come to the conclusion it would not harm Rebecca's baby if Andy appeared to her instead of them telling her about him. The shock would be a shock whichever way they did it.

Jim asked, "Will we both go over to her condo and be with her when he appears at her door?"

"I think we can soften the blow a little. When Andy knocks on the door, I'll suggest you go answer it for Rebecca. She'll think nothing of it. Andy can come in and stand behind her as she sits on the sofa. I'll make sure that's where she's seated by asking her to sit by me. Then Andy can say her name softly. God can take it from there!"

The plan was to go over to Rebecca's around two. Jim was sure it would take 'til then to get Andy released from the safe house, go by his apartment and let him change into some *real* clothes.

Beth had considerately moved the Redmon's clothes into the guest suite. Andy could come home and stay in his own room and have his apartment back; the Redmons planned to leave soon.

Sven was very nervous as he prepared for the meeting at Lockman's. Jim had suggested he come to their place to get ready. In that way, he wouldn't have to interact at all with his father. He left his father a note about why he wouldn't be home.

Beth prepared supper and the three sat down to eat. Before they were finished, Bruce appeared at their door. "I guess I felt like I had to be here in case Sven needed some moral support." He touched Sven's shoulder. The young man looked up with an expression of gratitude. Jim was touched as he realized his life had been sparse when it came to any loving interaction with a man. Jim also recognized the bond that had formed between the two since Katarina's arrival and subsequent death. The thought walked through his mind, *Maybe the two would remain friends after this nightmare was over.*

When the hour had arrived, Bruce stood in front of Sven and grabbed his hand. "I just want you to know that we all care what happens to you tonight. I've done everything I know to keep you safe. Just go in there with self-confidence and assurance that everything will be okay. We've got your back!"

Jim slapped Sven on the back and said, "We'll be thinking of you. You've already been briefed about how you'll be taken to FBI Headquarters with the others; then separated from them and released."

Beth stepped up to him and put her arms around him. "And I'll be praying for you non-stop."

Sven's eyes pooled with tears. "That means a lot to me. My mom said those same words to me the last time I was with her." He turned and left the apartment.

41.
The Final Meeting

Lockman had the explosives hidden in his office. They were separated into five different backpacks. . .all different styles. He was excited but a little nervous, very proud to be the one to give these patriots their instructions.

The men arrived within ten minutes of each other. None of them were close friends but were mere acquaintances. Sven looked at these men and wondered how he could have become an integral part of what they had planned.

Lockman stood before them in the living room. The rhetoric he used had its desired effect on the group, energizing them to a fevered pitch. Sven gave another Academy Aware performance. When Lockman finished his oratory, they were ready to follow Allah, off a cliff if need be.

"Now to prepare you for your task, I will instruct each of you individually as to where you are to place your backpack." A map was unfolded and each man was given his instructions and asked if he had any questions. When he came to Sven, he gave him a quick once-over looking for any sign of betrayal. Sven looked him right in the eye, as Jim had instructed. Lockman told him that his backpack was to be hidden in the kitchen as close to the dining room as possible. It turned Sven's stomach when he thought of how unconcerned the man was directing all of them to plant a bomb amidst so many innocent people.

Lockman took the group into his office and handed each one a backpack. As he was handing them out, he gave instructions. "These bombs are all wired to go off at a predetermined time. Before you go into the Terminal, flip this switch and the timer begins. The first bomb will be placed by you on the lower level," he said, as he handed the young man his backpack. As he handed out the rest, he said, "The last one will be detonated at the front door." He turned to Sven, "I want you to stay in position until after the first bomb goes off. When panic starts, the people in your restaurant will rush for the elevators and stairway. You are to take the service elevator in the back of the kitchen. Make your way as inconspicuously as possible when you hear the first explosion."

He turned to the others, "I want you to leave the moment you have put your bomb in place. Do *not* wait around."

Sven was alarmed when he knew his would-be escape had been delayed well after his bomb had been placed and he wasn't instructed to leave like the others. He knew in his gut that even though they had been assured of his allegiance, they were leaving nothing to chance. After all, a question had been raised concerning his loyalty; he was *supposed* to be caught in the confusion. He wondered when the bomb in the restaurant was truly to be detonated. He was happy he didn't have to worry about it.

They all carried their packs into the living room and Lockman again whipped them up into a frenzy, ending with complimenting them for their loyalty. The meeting was adjourned.

The moment Sven got in his truck, he called Bruce. "We've been dismissed. Where do you want me to go?"

"Head toward your apartment. We'll know soon enough whether someone is following you. Everyone in the group has someone following them and they'll be arrested on their way home. As we told you before, you will be taken into custody and brought to headquarters with the others to dispel any questions about your loyalty.

The operation went smoothly. Each and every man was arrested on their way home and had their backpacks confiscated. All of them were taken to the FBI where they were put in separate cells. They asked for their phone call, but was told it would have to wait. Bruce promised Sven he would release him as soon as they felt it was safe, which he did post-haste.

An agent knocked on Lockman's door. He opened the door, saying, "Now what?" before he realized it wasn't one of his men. The agent pushed his way in and was followed by a team of agents.

"You're under arrest for treason, Mr. Lockman." He was read his rights and handcuffed. The look on Lockman's face was priceless. The men swarmed into the office, confiscating the computer, files, map and anything they thought could be of value. One agent bent down and retrieved the listening device on the leg of the desk, and another agent removed the one in the living room. They shoved all trash from baskets into a large leaf bag, and different agents were told to check out every room in the house.

They were out of there in a matter of thirty minutes.

Bruce and his team went to Houseman's palatial home. They rang the doorbell and the butler answered. When he saw two well-dressed men on the thresh hold, he knew it didn't bode well for his boss. The agent stated they would like to speak with Mr. Houseman. The man ushered them into the vestibule and knocked on the study door telling Mr. Houseman he had guests. When he came out of his study, he saw the agents and suspected why they were there.

"What is this?" he blustered with bravado.

Bruce replied calmly, "We're here to place you under arrest for treason, Mr. Houseman. Whatever you say will . . ." Bruce read him his rights as he cuffed him.

Houseman told his butler to call his lawyer, then asked. "Where are you taking me?"

"To FBI Headquarters," said Bruce as he ushered the man out of his house.

The team of agents who were waiting by their cars, rushed through the door. The woman that was the FBI plant, showed the men where the lever was hidden to open Houseman's secret office. They swarmed over the place, leaving nothing unturned. They were *not* finished in thirty minutes. This would probably take hours and maybe a day or two. After arriving downtown, Lockman and Houseman were also held in separate cells.

When Bruce freed Sven, he slapped the young man on his back and praised him for his performance. The two ended up in the conference room.

"Now can we arrest my father?" Sven pleaded.

Bruce was a little surprised that he was adamant about putting his father under arrest so quickly. "Yes. I need to call Bob Stevens as he'll have to make the arrest." He immediately called Bob and then Jim, asking them to come to headquarters and he'd fill them in on the activities of the evening. It was forty-five minutes before they all arrived.

Manny was asked to come with Jim. The four men sat around the table celebrating the fact they had destroyed and neutralized the terrorist's plans. After a reasonable time, Bruce asked Bob if they were ready to arrest Abadi for murder.

"We have all our evidence, and it's solid. We also have Jamaal in a holding cell, and to save himself from being charged as an accessory to murder, he has agreed to give testimony about taking Ahmed to the Nobel Hotel. So, yes, we're more than ready."

Sven breathed a sigh of relief. "I'd like to see his face when he is charged."

Bob thought a moment and said, "We'll see what we can arrange."

Sven asked Jim to step outside of the conference room while he called Katarina's father. When the phone was answered, he said, "Grandfather?"

There was silence on the other end. Then a whispered, "Yes." Sven tried to continue, but he began to weep. He handed the phone to Jim.

"Sir, my name is Jim Redmon and I hate to be the bearer of bad news, but I'm sad to tell you that your daughter, Katarina, was murdered."

Silence.

Bruce came into the hall. He put his arm around Sven's shoulder and drew him over to a bench near the wall.

The old gentleman asked, "How?"

"The murder was committed by her ex-husband, Ahmed Abadi."

Mr. Knutzen could hardly speak, but managed to ask, "May I speak to my grandson?"

"Of course." Jim went over and handed the phone back to Sven. "He would like to speak to you."

The two spoke for at least five minutes, with Sven giving him a short version of what had happened. He said he could explain better when he saw him. Sven asked, "Can you come to New York right away, grandfather? Your plane ticket has been covered," he glanced at Jim with a look of gratitude. He then supplied Mr. Knutzen with his phone number as well as Jim's.

When Sven hung up, he explained that his grandfather would get a flight as soon as possible. He promised to call Sven with his flight plans.

Jim took Sven home with him. Beth was full of questions and wanted to know if all was arranged for Andy to come home. He told her that was way down on his list today; they would talk tomorrow. Sven fell into bed and slept soundly. Jim wasn't so lucky.

42.
Andy's Destiny

Bruce Foster had a long talk with Bob Stevens about the arrest of Ahmed Abadi. Both decided it would be safe for Sven to help them with his father's arrest.

Early the following morning, Jim and Manny went down to Bob's office. He was waiting for them and explained to them what the plan was for Ahmed's arrest. He explained how Sven agreed to wear a wire, go home, and put on another Academy Award performance.

Sven walked into the apartment purposefully leaving the door unlocked. His father lit into him, "Where've you been. You could have at least called!"

Sven answered with disdain, "Father, I'm twenty-four years old! I didn't know I was still on a curfew!"

Ahmed settled down some. "Where were you?"

"I was taking care of business. What have *you* been doing?"

This retort angered Ahmed further but for some reason he was afraid to confront Sven any further. Something was different about his son.

Sven sat down on the sofa. His father was preparing to go to work and he needed to move things along. "I found out what happened to my mother."

Ahmed jerked to attention. "What?"

"She was murdered in her hotel room! It didn't appear to be a robbery; it was personal." Sven stood up and began to pace the small room. "I got to thinking, who would want my mother dead? And you know what, father, your name was the only one I could come up with."

Ahmed started sputtering. "What are you talking about? I didn't even know where she was staying!"

Sven cut his eyes over to him. "Yes, you *did* know. I left you a note the other morning and told you myself."

"That doesn't mean I killed her. Anyway, how would I get into her room?"

"Oh that was easy." And Sven revealed what the police had learned from their investigation and the missing key-card from the maid's locker room.

To say Ahmed was surprised was an understatement. "I didn't even go to her hotel and I have a witness for all afternoon."

"Who said anything about *all afternoon?* So if you're referring to your good friend, Jamaal, he's in police custody singing his heart out."

The father didn't know what to say. He fell into a chair, saying, "I didn't mean to kill her. Just to scare her into leaving New York. It was an accident; I didn't want to lose you, son."

Sven spat, "You are one sorry piece of you know what! You took my mother away from me *twice.* I knew you hated her and wanted your revenge. Well, you got it. But I've got mine, too."

With that, the police barged in and arrested Ahmed.

When Jim got up Friday morning, he called Bruce to see if releasing Andy was still planned for Saturday. Bruce told him all that needed to be done was for the doctor to sign the papers. He asked Jim if he'd like to ride out with him Saturday morning to bring Andy home.

"Yes! For sure. I'll go through his closet and bring him some clothes. I presume the clothes he had on were ruined."

"I think the only thing worth saving was his shoes."

Beth had lunch ready and called Jim to come get it. He sauntered into the kitchen and the two bantered back and forth about the case.

Jim's phone rang, and it was Sven. "What can I do for you, son?"

Sven seemed to hem-haw around and finally blurted it out, "I have to remain in seclusion for a while longer. Could you do me a favor and pick up my grandfather at the airport?"

"Sure. When's he arriving?"

"I'm supposed to pick him up at four-thirty tomorrow." He supplied the name of the airline and told him he had arranged to meet his grandfather in Baggage.

"I can do that," agreed Jim. "What do I owe you for your grandfather's ticket?"

Sven was proud to answer, "He took care of it but wanted me to tell you thanks anyway."

Jim was glad he had thought ahead. "I rented a room at our old hotel for your grandfather. If Bruce says it's okay, it'd be nice if you could spend the time there until you two have made arrangements for your mother's release."

Sven was delighted and handed the phone over to Bruce. "Jim wants to ask you a question."

The following day, Jim and Bruce went out to pick up Andy. All had been resolved and Bruce was permitted to pick him up early on Saturday morning. On the way back, the two lawmen filled Andy in on how they squelched the terrorist's plans, and the arrest of Ahmed Abadi.

Andy asked Bruce if they could go by Tiffany's to pick up Rebecca's ring as he had made arrangements the day before. "The manager was shocked I was still alive and said he'd feel better if I came in person; the ring was very expensive." Andy had called Jim to bring his checkbook, so on their way home Bruce swung by Tiffany's and Andy went in to get the ring.

When Andy walked into his apartment, Beth was seated on the lush sofa. She rose to give him a hug. "Easy does it, honey," Jim cautioned. "He's still a little fragile."

Beth got the two men a mug of coffee and they all sat down for Andy to get his wind; he still tired easily. She told the men she had made arrangements for them to go over to Rebecca's around 1:30 pm. Andy was antsy, but surprisingly asked Jim to call his barber, "to see if he can cut my hair this morning. I want to appear as dashing as possible for my intended."

Jim went into Andy's office and called the barber. Yes, he'd *make* time for Andy; but he was full of questions. Jim laughed, "You'll have to ask the man himself when he gets there." The two men left, in Andy's truck.

Beth had sandwiches made when the men got back. They ate and readied themselves to go over to Rebecca's. Andy was as nervous as a cat. The threesome did as they planned earlier. They were in Rebecca's apartment when Andy rang the bell and Jim answered it. She never even looked around, thinking it was another delivery with more baby stuff.

As Jim entered the sitting area and sat down, Andy walked over to stand behind Rebecca. He quietly said, "Rebecca." She whirled around and couldn't believe her eyes.

"Wha. . . Is that *you* Andy?" She was shocked and Beth was glad she was sitting down. He left his cane hooked on the back of the sofa and limped around to face her. There were tears streaming down her cheeks as he sat next to her, gathering her into his arms.

"There, there, sweetheart. It's okay, and I'm okay." His eyes were tearing up, also.

"Before I explain anything to you, I have something to tell you." He gained control; "I love you! I planned to do this before I was abducted, so it was put on hold." He reached into his pocket and got the ring and spoke ever so softly, "I've never said these words to anyone before, but I hope you love me and will agree to be my wife."

Rebecca was still in shock from seeing Andy, but this was more than she ever bargained for. She threw her arms around his neck and blubbered into his neck, "Of course I love you and I'd be honored to be your wife."

Beth motioned to Jim and they left. As much as she wanted to hear how Rebecca told Andy she was pregnant, she felt it was a time for them to be alone.

As they drove back to Andy's, Jim said, "I made a reservation for us to return home the end of next week."

"Why so long?" she asked.

"Andy asked me if I'd be his best man and I'm sure you'll be Rebecca's matron of honor. We talked about it and he thinks he can get the license and all by Wednesday. And I just *knew* you and Rebecca would want to shop for a bridal outfit!"

Beth was so excited that she unbuckled her seatbelt and snuggled close to her wonderful husband, smooching his neck.

Jim summed it all up. "I guess the whole lousy situation led up to this day for Andy to get the wife of his dreams and a baby on the way." The two laughed.

That evening, Andy called Jim to tell him the good news. "I'm going to be the father of a baby girl! He was jubilant and added, "And we're going to call her Destiny."

About the Authors

J A Smith is a voracious reader of all types of literature. "My favorite genre is mysteries and action novels," says Smith. A participant in golf in years past, Smith found the sport consumed too much time. Hence, travel, family, and painting have become three favorite pastimes. This is Smith's second novel, preceded by *Redmon's Raiders*.

Curtis Smith is new to the writing scene. An avid athlete with a passion for golf and basketball, his health issues have curtailed his participation in all sports. He continues to work at his floor-covering business and enjoys his free time traveling, reading, puzzles and poker.

The two Smith's conspired together to write *37 Days to Destiny;* an engaging sequel to *Redmon's Raiders*. The first novel was J. A. Smith's first attempt to write a book. It was about six ex-military buddies, who remained friends after their tour, and how they joined together to find their kidnapped comrade. The pursuit drives them from Chattanooga to Atlanta and Miami. Drugs, murder and greed hinder the Raiders throughout their hair-raising quest.

Many readers asked when the sequel would be out, which brought about the second novel, *37 Days to Destiny*. Smith is hopeful this novel will be as well received as the first. If so, there may be a third!

Made in the USA
Charleston, SC
22 December 2015